COLONY

a one-shot anthology of speculative fiction

Compiled by David F. Shultz

TDOTSPEC

Colony: a one-shot anthology of speculative fiction
Compiled by David F. Shultz

Published by tdotSpec Inc.
ISBN# 978-1-9994039-4-2

Interior design and cover design by David F. Shultz
Cover Illustration "Desert Planet" © 2013-2018 Joakim Olofsson

ACKNOWLEDGEMENTS

This anthology is the second of our "one-shot" anthologies. It is the product of an intense, one-day period of writing and editing by a team of writers currently residing in Toronto. The anthology was a joint effort between the *Toronto Science Fiction and Fantasy* writers group and the *Toronto Horror Writers* group. I would like to thank all of the writers for contributing their talent and time in order to make this anthology possible. Thanks, everyone! It was a lot of fun, and we created something awesome, thanks to you!

I would like to thank Mitchell, "The Itch", who runs the *Toronto Horror Writers* group. Mitchell helped organize the event, and originally suggested the idea. He also brought members of his *Toronto Horror Writers* group to add a touch of darkness to the collection. Thanks, Mitchell, and thanks, horror writers!

And I would also like to thank the reader, whoever you may be, for taking a chance on this anthology. I hope you enjoy the stories and find the collection interesting. Thanks for reading!

David F. Shultz

INTRODUCTION

This is the second of our "one-shot" anthologies. The idea is to challenge ourselves to create an entire anthology in a single day. This feat requires exceptional focus and productivity, since creating an anthology usually takes about a year.

We do this in part for the challenge and in part to see what we can come up with. There's also an added element of fun to reading these stories, knowing the extreme conditions under which they were produced.

For this anthology, all of the writers were given the theme "Colony" in advance. Writers were allowed to plan their idea beforehand based on this theme. But all the writing and editing was done in a single day, most of it over four hours in a marathon writing session at *The Imperial Pub* in downtown Toronto.

The first time we did this, I was expecting the average length of stories to be around 1 to 1.5 thousand words, which is a professional rate for a good day's work. The average length turned out to be 2,130 words, with 23 works totalling 49,000 words. This time, by sheer coincidence, we again hit the 49,000 mark, but with only 17 works total. The average output from writers on this anthology was 2800 words!

Some of the writers have included author notes with their contributions to give additional insight into their stories and/or perspective into the writing process.

We didn't exert any editorial or quality control over the final product. The only requirement was that the stories be legal, with the most likely illegality being copyright infringement. Beyond that, anything that was written by our participating writers made it in.

The stories appear in the order in which they were received.

Since writing and editing was strictly limited to a 24-hour window, you're likely to find more spelling and grammatical errors than a typical anthology, more awkward phrasings, and more chaff, which is usually cut during editing.

I guarantee that this is not the most polished anthology out there. But I also guarantee that it is a fun and interesting read. This is more than a collection of imaginative and entertaining stories—it is also a feat in creative writing. It embodies the efforts of authors writing and editing fervently under absurd time pressures. They set themselves a challenge and pushed themselves to the finish line. This book is the result of their efforts, and it's awesome.

I hope you have fun reading *Colony*!

David F. Shultz

CONTENTS

OUTTA SIGHT

Amad Raven

There is no sense of time here. No morning. No night. But the light is blinding and bright, minus the warmth of the sun. Just think bone cold.

Yeah… no one wants to be here.

The Briefing

"Okay. Okay, we all here?" Gus pans the legion. "Where's Smitty? Any of you lock eyes on Smitty?"

"He's still out on assignment with his crew," Kal roars.

"Hey, I'm the upset one here, so take it down a notch, Kal."

Gus surveys the legion. It's an ugly bunch for sure: tall waifs, fatties with leaky puss, sickly-yellow ones with ancient burns, and gigantic furries. Some have wings. Most do not.

"So, we're doing great… sorta. But the Boss is gettin' edgy, he's gonna kick it up. Clocks tickin'. Can you hear it?" Gus raises his ear to the distant sound of a choir. It's a dress rehearsal, there's laughter, lots of laughter. And they're itching to party down.

The legion gets spooked. That's the last thing you wanna hear, because it will for sure be the last thing you do hear.

"Settle down. Everyone, calm yourselves. They've been waiting centuries for it, and it's not happening any time soon. But the Boss has upped the quota."

Gus reads through his parchment. "Where's Eddie?"

Eddie raises a furry paw.

"Eddie, you gotta speak up. You're all whispers, what's with that? Let's pretend you're at an Aerosmith concert, cause Grandpa never whispered. He was loud raging drunk. So next time Madame What's Her Face starts groanin', make it sound real, cause I wasn't convinced."

"Got it."

"Okay. So, Spanks, you here…" Gus searches the crowd. "Hey, Bobby, move over will you. Anyone got eyes on Spanks? I know he's here. I can smell him."

"Right in front of you, boss," Spanks waves.

"Man, I gotta get my eyes checked. Shit. Okay, so what happened at Sally's slumber party? You totally missed the mark. I mean they had the board out, they were all freaked out from watching that bullshit movie – the opportunity was ripe. And where were you? M.I.A. is where."

"I was watching the neighbour."

"Exactly! You left your assignment and stepped on Johnny's beat, and Johnny let you. That's why the both of you now got two strikes. And what happens after three…"

Fevered chatter rushes through the crowd.

"What happens? C'mon, let's hear it."

"The cage, Sir!" a wee voice answers.

"What? I can't hear you?"

"THE CAGE!" they roar in one voice.

"Right. And we don't want that. Shit, no we don't. Pete's still in there, bored out of his mind, watching the choir rehearse. Like, forget that. Shoot me now."

Gus scrolls through the parchment. "There's more, lots more, but I'll let it pass, for now. My ass is on the line, just you know, which means your ass is mine. Just do your assignments. Meeting's over. Now scat."

The legion disperses in varied directions. Gus reads through the rest of the list, and it's damn long. He dreads what will happen next. He actually hates it. Oh, how he hates it.

Meet the Big Boss

"Enter."

Gus steps into a white shag carpeted den. It's covered in bronze and imitation gold. There's windows for walls, except one wall that's covered in endless screens showing the mundane lives of people living their day to day.

"Hey, Boss, how's it going?"

"I told you to call me, Sam, didn't I?" Sam paces feverishly, eyeing one screen in particular.

"Yeah, sure, but I wanna keep it formal. You know, me being me, you being you and all."

"Let's call this your second warning," Sam smirks.

"Right, Sam. Got it."

"I take it the meeting went well. Everyone accomplishing their assignments?"

"We're on the ball, we're good. All is good."

"Good? Good, you say…" Sam throws his head back in hysterical laughter. He then lurches forward, bracing himself, eyeing the screen in disbelief. He then turns and glares to Gus.

"You okay? Can I get you anything?" Gus swallows hard.

Sam eyes the screen trying to hold back the rage. Droplets of blood fall from his forehead, hitting the ground. Gus tucks his parchment under his scaly wing. He tries to see the screen in question.

"You see this? This SHIT!" Sam walks up to the screen.

"Yeah, that's that show L-"

"Stop right there. Don't even finish that word. You do and I'll send you straight to the cage." Sam wipes his bloody forehead.

"Shutting up."

"This is a problem." Sam smears his blood on the screen. "Do you know what I look like here, right here? Do you!"

Gus stays silent. He dare not say a word.

"I look like a fool. A fool in love," Sam grits his teeth, smearing a circle around a man's face.

"Is this a new assignment?"

Sam strides quickly, standing inches from Gus's face. He smears his blood on Gus's forehead. "I'm sticky and gooey, like syrup, like candy. I'm the good guy!" his eyes bulge." Bring me home to mommy why don't you!" he laughs a horrified laugh.

"So…."

"Give Tom a visit… we need to terminate his contract." Sam walks away.

"Who's Tom?"

Author's Note

It was supposed to be longer. This is a snippet of the B story to the original.

COLONIZE THIS!

Christopher Donald Griffin

In the darkness of the cave, Calliper sank deeper and deeper into the ooze. It squirmed around his slick folds, seeped into his pours, and sloshed in and out of his delicate gills. A tingling sensation erupted throughout his young form.

Calliper opened his eyes. The ooze slid gently against the membrane of his outer-eyes. The green glow of the "Lake of Life" filled not just his vision, but his very imagination. He remembered all the times, over the course of his life, the daydreams he would indulge in. When his time came, and the transformation had commenced, he imagined what he might come out looking like.

Imagination was a unique and celebrated trait amongst his people, the Goeotes. Only one in a thousand spawn were born with the ability to dream and ponder at what might be. Only the few could see beyond the role the All-Mother endowed them with. These rare beings, these Ramatodes, were both praised and feared, for they were born with the potential to create but also to destroy; and they had the power to choose which destiny they embraced.

As he sank further, and pain began to shoot through every cell in his body, Calliper remembered back.

He was spawn number 2 785 in a brood of ten thousand. The apple of the All-Mother's many eyes. He was one of four of nine Ramatodes to survive cannibalism by the brood. Sibling rivalry, Calliper chuckled through searing pain, what a silly thing.

He loved his siblings, he really did. For mindless drones, they were alright. They were dedicated, efficient, productive, and obedient. Could you ask for anything more in a family unit? Calliper didn't think so. He sometimes envied them. While he was consumed with inner conflict, pondering the significance of existence and the purpose of life, they were doing an honest day's work, such as building nests out of the All-Mother's viscous and gelatinous excrements. Calliper was terrible at nest building. He didn't possess the delicate touch required for excremental sculpting and finishing.

The colony he was born into had inhabited these caves for millions of cycles. The brood travelled, it grew, it travelled, and it grew. Expansion and growth, the corner stone of a sustainable economy. Something to be proud of.

Ramatodes, like Calliper, served a special purpose within the brood. They served as scouts. As the colony expanded into the territory of new species, it was the Ramatodes' purpose to assume the form of the competitor organism, learn their ways, assess their weaknesses, and prepare the brood for invasion.

This led the Goeote colony to their current situation. Calliper, was born with one extra special trait, the ability to detect objects by utilizing reflected light, a resource in short supply in their world. This defect nearly justified the cannibalism of Calliper as a larva, had it not been for the discovery of "Infinite Space" or as the All-Mother described it "The cavern with no end". A place where sound waves stretched out into infinity.   A land flooded with light.

The dominant species was a disorganized, erratic, and confusing brood. Leadership was inconsistent, roles shifted almost daily, and drones could spawn their own drones. It was a land ruled by anarchy, a land the All-Mother wished to purge of chaos, and Calliper would play a key role in that purge.

Calliper became one with the ooze. His carapace sank into his flesh, his mandibles became segmented, forming two orderly rows. His lineage identification glands burst free from his lower abdomen, as they merged and became elongated and worm-like. He grew a new skin; soft but dry. All at once, his chest constricted, oxygen had been cut off from his blood stream. How could this be?

Calliper burst free from the ooze. He crawled up onto the rocks. Their usual warm and silky texture had become hard and rough. The worm like appendage protruding from his abdomen, scraped against the stone bringing with it an ungoeote level of pain. He rolled onto, what he assumed was now his back, and let out a cry.

His cry was answered by echoes of his brethren's violent and defensive chirps. They no longer recognized him. Heaving in his chest, Calliper arose onto new chunky-soft limbs and set off into a run. His senses had become dull, but his memory was as sharp as ever. The All-Mother's shared memories of the route to the "Cavern with no end" shot into his mind. He followed the All-Mother's instincts.

He climbed rocks, squeezed through tunnels, and raced through caverns. The closer he came to his destination, the easier his breaths came to him and the greater warmth he felt enter his new form.

It came upon him all at once, a sea of light. He collapsed into it; his chest burning and his body limp.

Exhausted, Calliper lie on a bed of the greenest creatures he had ever laid eyes on. The organism was made up of long and crisp blades that tickled his soft skin. They grew out of the softest ground he had ever touched. Calliper peered up towards the ceiling of the cavern... there was no ceiling... just blue... a wall of blue reaching out into the distance in every direction.

Creatures, similar in appearance to his new form, peered down at him. One poked his worm with a stick. They all wore identical uniforms, hats, and scarves. They were all half his size. One, with lines of metal in his mouth hugging tiny white mandibles together, stood up straight and proud. He must be their All-Mother. The creature uttered strange sounds.

"Dude, put on some pants!"

Calliper couldn't understand a word the creature said, but it sounded friendly.

"Somebody get this retard a blanket and go find Scouter Carl. Just don't stand there idiots, do you want this drunk's death on your conscious?"

A couple of other creatures ran off. The one with the metal braces removed his scarf and tossed it over Calliper's worm.

"I'm too young for this shit! Just so you know, if you try anything, we've got knives. I earned my coon skinning badge last month. I'm just saying."

Calliper felt bad that this noble creature was exerting so much effort in an attempt to communicate with him, and all he could do was stare up at him. This was his moment, his purpose come to life. First contact, it was happening.

Calliper opened his mouth, with high hopes as to what was to come "Num num bra slamma robba liclife opopoopoo Clllliiikkkk *burp*".

Another one of the small creatures commented on what Calliper himself considered a sweet and poetic introduction.

"He sounds just like my uncle, only half as drunk."

Calliper grinned skin flap to skin flap.

•

Ten years passed, as Calliper worked hard to integrate himself into the world of humanity. What was once a strange and chaotic world of infinite space, was now home.

Calliper stretched out his arms and legs. The bed beneath him was damp, stained, and riddled with bugs. Dirt and cigarette burns covered the room's carpets with a collage of misuse. The ceiling was no less stained. Half the lamps were burned out, and the toilet groined like an old diabetic man in a candy store.

Friends often asked Calliper whether he was "crazy or just stupid". He had money enough to stay in the finest five star hotels, and yet, he stayed in $30 a night motel rooms. They would tell him "This place is disgusting!" and Calliper would reply "Exactly!"

"Hey baby, have you seen my sugar?" came a voice from out of the bathroom. Calliper turn his head in time to see Lucy exit the bathroom, dressed in nothing but a g-string and a tube-top. She was a vision: round "engineered" breasts, long legs, greasy hair... a ribcage you could play like a xylophone, and a tattoo of a grizzled old sailor on her left ass-cheek. To Calliper, this woman was sheer perfection.

Lucy asked again "Hun! Have you seen my sugar?"

Calliper replied with "Have you checked your arm?"

Lucy looked down and finally noticed the syringe stuck in and dangling from her pencil thin arm. Without flinching, she pulled it out, as a huge grin burst onto her face. "Thank you darling, you're the best!"

He grinned back at her. This was his life now. Friends told him he needed to clean up his life, he had so much potential, but that his way of life was disgusting. Calliper loved that word "disgusting", for him, it was a promise of good things to come. Disgusting food, was the best of food. Disgusting habits, were the best of habits. Lucy's frothy discharge, she called a medical condition, but to Calliper, it was ecstasy. Calliper drank the kool-aid, and he would never go back.

His first couple of years among mankind were confusing and painful, but he learned one thing in his time with them, the prize went to those willing to do what other's weren't willing to do.

His rags to riches story began with a simple video uploaded to the internet. He was the first person on record to chug two litres of bleach, in less than five seconds, not puke, and live. A couple of weeks of blindness, rectal bleeding, and random blackouts were worth the price of his rise to stardom.

Having grown up surrounded by drones, Calliper had learned the value of hard work and a "can do" attitude. Before money started flowing; Calliper was more than willing to clean toilets, dispose of medical supplies, transport and bury nuclear waste, and change diapers at a local nursing home. The residents at the nursing home taught Calliper that the end of one's life could be spent with grace and dignity. Humans didn't cannibalize their dying and feeble, this was something he respected.

His favourite activity came from discussing philosophy, politics, and religion at the local shelter. The ideas that came out of these wise old men's mouths blew his mind.

To Calliper, life on the surface was a buffet, and he didn't have to share it with millions of drones. He could have it all to himself. Anything he wanted, could be his. He was his own Goeote. He learned the ways of capitalism. Most of all, he loved Wall Street, where you could own shares that you weren't obligated to share. He revelled in the irony.

The highlight of his career was when he ended up on the cover of "Forbes Magazine" under the title "The Most Wonderful

Horrible Person on the Planet".

His life was a fantasy, that is, until the "Calling" hit him one night. He was dressed in his fanciest tuxedo, out on the town, sharing some discarded fried chicken with a family of raccoons, when the sensation struck him. The All-Mother was calling him home. He could feel her pheromones in every pore and orifice of his body.

For the first time in his three hundred and sixty two year life, Calliper was happy, he didn't want to go home. Once Lucy had received her pardon and was taken off the sexual offenders list, he was going to whisk her away to the Congo for a romantic jungle wedding. She was always asking him "What's your poison?" so he chose a destination where the options for poisons were endless. He could try them all!

His old friend, inner conflict, began to torment Calliper. It was his life's purpose to educate his brood on the movements and defences of opposition species. He was born to conquer. The All-Mother was calling to him, and the clock was ticking. He peered down at his new emerald studded Rolex watch. The precious gems twinkled with the same deep green as the ooze had once done, when it had changed him. He was born to conquer, and since he had come to the surface, conquer he did. Up here, he was a king. Up here, his only equal were the wild dreams that lived within him, since as long as he could remember. To live amongst drones, as a drone, answering to a single power, was no life for a Goeote with imagination and ambition. Born to create or destroy... or maybe both at once.

He thought of all the friends he had made, their unique personalities, struggles, and beliefs. He thought of the chaos he had learned to embrace and truly and deeply love. He thought of Lucy's frothy discharge, and it's sweet aroma.

There could be only one solution.

•

One hundred and fifty seven years later. Although human in appearance, Calliper aged with the uneventful stagnation of a Goeote. Other than a few grey hairs, he didn't appear a day older than that first moment he had dragged his soft new form out of the glowing ooze.

His two decades of marriage to Lucy had been as beautiful as they had been turbulent. After the delivery of seven still-born children – humans and goeotes cannot successfully interbreed – Calliper and Lucy decided to adopt a pair of Norwegian twins they named Christopher and Glop. Two years later, Lucy died of a tragic heroin overdose. He buried her in her favourite garden, where no one would find the body. He knew humans didn't consume their dead... but one couldn't be too careful.

Calliper went into politics, partially to distract him from grief felt over his wife's passing, and partially because the inane arguing of fellow politicians helped to drown out the All-Mother's calls that tormented him day and night.

There was only one way to finally answer the All-Mother's summons, he had to return to the brood, to serve his purpose, once and for all.

In the depths of the All-Mother's subterranean nest, towering thirty feet tall and then some, she looked down over her lovely brood of drones. Legions of larva suckled on the viscous discharges released from her massive and engorged abdomen.

Calliper stood before her, proud, determined, and housed in a brand new twenty foot tall military-grade suit of mechanized armour. Calliper offered his thoughts to his All-Mother "Turn back, the cavern with no end is not your's to have."

She replied, "All things belong to the All-Mother. To the brood."

During all his years on the surface, Calliper had become an avid fan of popularly culture, comic books in particular, and it never ceased to amaze him how many fictional super-villains reminded him of the All-Mother.

Calliper finally answered "How cliche".

"What?" said the All-Mother.

"You heard me!" he shot back.

With a sad sigh, Calliper typed a command into the controls of his suit. His suit's right arm raised up into the air, canon pointed directly at the All-Mother's head. One shot, and her life was over.

The army of drones stood still, and looked about in confusion, not a single one moved from it's spot.

Calliper addressed his siblings, "My family, long have we been separated, both by distance, and by culture. Today I offer you all the depths have to offer, you are free from control. Your fate is your own."

At that, Calliper turned away for a brood that was once his home, and began his long trek back to the surface.

•

One hundred years passed.

Down within the caverns.

The All-Mother's nest lay near frozen in time. Her massive corpse rotting away. All of the drones lay dead, of inaction and starvation, in the exact same spots they stood, the day Calliper had "liberated" them. The stench of their rot filled the caverns.

On the surface.

Calliper stood behind a podium, before an audience of hundreds of young hopefuls. A massive state-of-the-art auditorium surrounded him. He addressed the students of his new "School of Free Thoughts".

"My children, I created this school with a vision for a better future. A future where all of mankind will have the opportunity to not only dream, but to pursue those dreams as best they can. This school is for those willing to challenge the status quo and to rise to new heights. I only ask one thing of each and everyone of you. I ask you to tell me to go fuck myself and run off and do your own thing."

The students looked about at each other in confusion.

Calliper continued "You'll figure it out, as I did. Now, if you'll excuse me, I have a hooker waiting for me in the honeymoon suite at 'Groover's Motor Hotel' and if I don't get there in time, she'll be forced to punish me."

The audience gasped.

"One more thing" Calliper added "Life's a buffet, eat it up!"

He dropped the mic, and exited the stage.

Author's Note

I wrote this at the end of a crazy week, with some erratic sleep patterns. Come tomorrow morning, I'll be lucky if I remember what I wrote. I apologize for any typos I overlooked.

FOR MANKIND

By Don Miasek

Anvi pressed the button next to the intercom. "Is it supposed to smell this bad?"

"The chemical composition of the atmosphere is within expected parameters." The heavily modulated voice from the speakers betrayed no hint as to his or her identity.

Anvi let go and backed into the center of her cell. Dark red vapour poured through the vents, blanketing the deck like a thick carpet. Anvi stood up straight, wanting to keep her head above the haze as long as she could.

You asked for this, she reminded herself. It was this or perma-labour, and Anvi had no desire of being stuck on some asteroid for the rest of her life. She paced back and forth. She had to take a leak, but sitting on the corner toilet would have meant putting her head beneath the rising fog.

Not that there seemed to be any way to avoid that for long. It was now up to her waist. Anvi stepped up to the intercom and held the button. "I'm serious, it smells really bad. Maybe there's a malfunction."

"Be strong and courageous. Do not be afraid or terrified, for we will never forsake you."

Asses, Anvi thought. Every one of the lab coats out there. Treating us all like goddamn animals. "Well can't you just inject this crap via my cybernetics?"

"We need to wean you off your cybernetics."

That took Anvi aback. "Already? I thought that wasn't for

another two weeks."

"The timetable has been moved up. The Directors have added additional stabilization time to the schedule."

"When?"

"All your cybernetics will be permanently deactivated in thirty hours."

Anvi opened her mouth in horror, but couldn't think of anything to say. Everything was happening so fast.

"Anvi Briere, your blood pressure is rising. Go to your bed. In peace you will lie down and sleep."

Anvi looked at the bed next to the toilet. "And breathe whatever junk you're pumping in here? No thanks, jackass." If you can smell it then you're already breathing it, a little voice told her. Anvi told that voice to shut up. The reddish fog was now up to her breasts.

"That was not a request. By order of Sentencing Committee 280, you are compelled. Go to bed."

Anvi let go of the intercom button and scowled. She wondered how much disobedience a prisoner could get away. They'd spent so much money that washing her out of the project didn't seem likely. Thank God for the law of coin, Anvi thought.

But maybe it'd be better this way. Maybe just ducking down and getting it over with was better than standing on tippy toes, or climbing onto the toilet, or whatever else she could think of to keep above the fumes. With a resigned sigh, Anvi marched over to the bed, sat down, and breathed deep.

•

The airlock next to the intercom rumbled, and Anvi jolted from her bed. How long was I asleep? It felt like days. The soupy red air

made it impossible to see further than an inch in front of her. Anvi
slid her hands along the wall, feeling her way past the corner toilet,
around the dresser with her only change of clothes, and all the way
to the door on the far side of her cell.

With some trial and error, she found the slit in the door and
pulled the newly arrived metal tray in with her. Her stomach was
already growling. When was the last time they fed me?

"Wait..." Anvi held the tray in one hand while she pressed the
intercom. "These aren't my normal rations."

"Your rations have been updated. Go, eat your food with
gladness."

"Why?" Anvi sniffed the tray. It had a sharp, stinging odour
to it. "Is this medicine?"

No answer.

"If it's medicine you have to tell me. By law you have to. It
says so right in my Settler's Agreement."

No answer.

Maybe it wasn't medicine, and so that's why they didn't have
to say anything. Anvi felt four little ovoid shaped chunks on the
tray. Were they pills?

"You know, I should speak to my lawyer. Fire up the
transmitter, dickholes. I have an official complaint to make.
 Convicts still have rights."

That got the voice going. "It is not medicine. These capsules
contain tissue nanites that will assist with the process."

"Sounds like medicine to me."

"By law, they are not medicine."

Anvi rubbed one of them between her thumb and forefinger.
It was squishy on the outside but firm within.

"Perhaps a consultation with a higher authority is indeed

needed."

Anvi shivered. Maybe she overestimated how much money they were willing to lose on her. Maybe they'd tell the Magistrate to revoke her sentence. That could mean something far worse than a little medicine. Anvi didn't like her chances of beating them in a legal argument.

One by one, Anvi put them into her mouth and swallowed.

•

"My head hurts," Anvi said. The pounding had been relentless. Just when she'd gotten used to the smell of the air, they'd added bright glaring lights that flashed at irregular intervals. Green, purple, yellow... they all made her eyes ache as they cut through the smog.

"Stand by."

Anvi wondered how many suits were out there manning the intercom. Though the computerized voice never changed, sometimes she thought its mannerisms did. Some were harsher than others. Maybe they took shifts in torturing her.

"Nothing unusual found," the voice said.

"Then why do I feel like someone is hammering the inside of my skull?" she snarled.

"Know that we have plans for you. Plans to prosper you and not to harm you. Plans to give you hope and a future."

Anvi winced as another blast of yellow light shot through the room. She tried to turn away, but that just prompted bursts from the other side. Anvi squeezed her eyes as tight as she could, but she swore she could see the damn things right through her eyelids.
 Anvi crouched down low to protect herself.

"Do not lose heart. Though outwardly you are wasting away, inwardly you are being renewed day by day," the voice said.

Keeping her head buried in her knees, Anvi reached up and held the button. "Please... I can't take any more of this."

"You will adapt."

"Please..." Another burst of light, and Anvi felt like her head was going to split in two. "I can barely think. Painkillers... or... or... sedation... or... this wasn't part of the plea bargain. I can't think straight anymore..."

The voice said nothing.

"If there's anything... uh... h-human in you, please help me." When there was no answer, Anvi let her hand fall from the intercom.

The slit in the airlock door slid open, and Anvi quickly grabbed the tray. In one fluid motion, she downed the handful of what she prayed were painkillers. Her head went light as she fell to the ground.

•

My clothes don't fit no more. Anvi scratched at the collar of her tunic. It was too tight around her neck. Maybe the smog had shrunk the fabric. The people out there must have turned down the atmospheric, because she was able to see a lot better now. Even the flashes of light didn't seem so bad.

The room was pretty ok... except for the clothes. Even her pants didn't feel right. Anvi pulled them down and wiggled them free of her feet. Her tunic quickly followed. Ah. Better. Her nakedness made her a lot more comfortable.

She expected the voice to come on and yell at her for indecent behavior, but that didn't happen. The suits out there were getting more laid back. Maybe the nice one was on shift today.

With that pleasant thought, Anvi curled up on the floor and

fell into a slumber.

•

"...and it is with this giant leap for mankind that you serve your sentence," the voice on the intercom said.

Anvi didn't really get what he was going on about. The suit had been talking about this kind of stuff for a while now.

"You will be fruitful. You will multiply."

Anvi wasn't sure what fruit or math had to do with anything.

"You will rule over the playcephaxenos in the murk and the ornithxenos in the air and over every living organism that moves terrestrially."

That's all fine and dandy, Anvi thought. Her stomach growled, and as if on cue the bright lights began flashing at the far corner. Anvi gleefully leapt across and stuck out her tongue. The purple was usually the best, but this time she had a hankering for yellow.

"Your service to mankind shall not be forgotten," the voice said.

"Hi?" Anvi said.

The voice went quiet the instant she spoke. Anvi no longer needed to press the round knob-thing next to the intercom to get them to hear her.

"Dunno why but it's harder to, um..." She fought for the word.

"With complex mental capacity comes complex psychology. It would be unsuited for the rigors of Epsilon Sigma Nine's environment."

"Oh. That's nice," Anvi said. She didn't quite it all she got the gist: they were looking out for her, and that was swell.

"An existence without normal stimuli would result in extreme boredom. Insanity would soon ensue."

"Mmhmm," Anvi said, not really listening anymore to all the tough-to-figure-out words. Instead she lapped the yellow fast as she could. When she had her fill, Anvi bounded back to her bed, clawed out a new sleeping hole, closed both sets of eyelids, and fell asleep.

•

Anvi cried in horror as the floor beneath her violently rose and fell. The entire world... or... ship? Boat? It must be tearing itself apart! She pressed herself against the weird metal bowl in the corner of her room--she had vague recollections of defecating in that spot--in a desperate attempt to stay on her feet as the room shook.

What was happening? Maybe the men and women making the voices had grown tired of her. Maybe they had decided to get rid of her!

Tears streamed down Anvi's face as she waited for the end. She wanted to beg them. I'll take the... the... medicine? The breathing? The... Anvi couldn't think of what she possibly could have done to upset them, so instead she stayed in her corner and cried.

Just when it seemed like the room was going to rip in two, the shaking stopped, leaving in its wake a gentle swaying. After some hesitation, Anvi crawled back into the middle of the room. She opened her mouth. Hi? She thought, but her tongue couldn't form the word.

The room violently shuddered once more, nearly knocking Anvi off her feet. But then it was perfectly still. She skittered over to the door. Hi?

She heard a creak on the far side, and to her amazement the

entire wall folded downward, revealing a world that looked so alien but felt so right. Its thick reddish air was instantly familiar to her as she stepped down into this strange new place.

There were other rooms, Anvi saw, that landed (yes, that was the word) not far from her own. She carefully approached one of them, gliding over the broken rocks of her new land. At first she did not recognize the grey hard substance that this box was made of, but it dawned on her that it was no different than her own chamber.

One of the walls fell with a crash, and out emerged a stunning being with a lithe frame, a thick neck, and a long elegant tongue that flicked in and out. His hide rippled with all the colours of the rainbow. He was beautiful.

Hi? thought Anvi.

Hi? he thought.

On the great rocks around her, Anvi saw the capsules open up one by one, and her fellow settlers came out to join them. There were soon hundreds, and Anvi had a vague sense that more of their brethren were scattered across the lands.

The sudden roar of distant thunder grabbed her attention. On the horizon, purple, green, and yellow lightning streaked down from the heavens. It would be a long journey to get there before the storm died out, but Anvi was hungry, determined, and knew she was not alone.

The flock broke into a run.

Author's Note

All too often, people scoff at the notion of sci-fi colonies on other planets by listing all the obstacles. Too much radiation on Mars. Lighter gravity would weaken our bones. The travel time would take too long.

We'd probably never be able to breathe the atmosphere. No supplies or infrastructure.

To all this I say: So what?

Humans have been smashing through obstacles since the first caveman bashed a rock with a club. This story was to illustrate just how far we may have to go. Will it be worth it?

SMELL THE MOOD ON THAT!

K. Connor

EXT CLOUDLESS BLUE SKY – DAY

The Sun beats white hot on a graffiti stained Colony helicopter. It sputters high above a massive red poppy field.

EXT DIRT HELI-PAD PATCH – DAY

A dust cloud sprays upward as the copter teeters into a soft landing. A capable friendly Woman (FUSHAY) jumps from the cockpit and jogs slightly out of wind range of the propellers.

EXT POPPY FIELD – DAY

It's quiet but for a slight wind. Red poppies roll out in large swatches like yoga mats on a desert colored wooden floor. Fushay inhales deeply through her nose.

                    FUSHAY
          Smell the mood on that!

She expertly unfolds a compacted Electric Scooter hidden in the poppy beds. Her boots slam dust on its' deck. Baby rubber scooter wheels' bunny hop on a barely visible dirt trail before they surf the red sea into a faraway tree line.

INT FARM HOUSE - DAY

Fushay is a blood hound. She palms piles of tied harvested yet fresh cut poppies ready for shipping. Allergic reactions would be dangerous in here.

BETH, an animated sharp eyed type Woman bounds down the stairs.

BETH

How's the harvest lookin'?

FUSHAY

All good from the Sky.

BETH

Smells strong, right?

FUSHAY

I love the stank! Guaranteed 90% of harvest, got the 100% scent.

BETH

That's what I like to hear. Confirm the order details now, K? I need a quick turn around on this.

                    FUSHAY
I have about 30% of orders sittin' without
deposit right now.

                    BETH
Why.

                    FUSHAY
My   guess?   Free   scent   zones   got'em
spooked. It's the new normal you know.

                    BETH
Copy that. Just make it happen, Fushay. K?
I'm counting on you.

                    FUSHAY
I got you.

Fushay's eye catches pockets of yellow dust that explode near her
head. She looks for the source.

BLAKE, 22 years of 'Nerd' stumbles in. He carries too many pots
of pollen tacked mustard weeds. A yellow trail of dust hovers the
tiles behind him.

                    BLAKE
The nasally challenged can numb down our
sense of smell BUT they won't succeed!
Down with the crusaders!

BETH

Amen!

FUSHAY

Amen? That's out of character.

BETH

Hey, agnostics can go to church sometimes. I'm just soap boxin'. ..Which if I remember was the reason why we started the Outpost in the first place. 'The Outpost is the safest place to be'. Right? That is what we said. To be out of the fray of the Colony ills. To soap boxin..

BLAKE

Uh Uh. That is what FUSHAY said. Refreshingly, I said, 'L'Occitane, is the safest place to be… Us, scent seekers need refuge. To lavender ..soap boxin..

Blake sniffs his underarms.

BLAKE

Yup, my pits still smell gooood. 36 hours later. My Snoz loves Mr. C. Klein.

FUSHAY

You're such a weirdo nerdo.

                    BLAKE
Remember when scent used to be about
sex? Which I adored. But now it's an
abomination. I would've never thought my
right to smell would become so
contentious that it'd become against the
law.

Fushay heads to the door.

                    BETH
Where's she goin'?

                  FUSHAY (O.S.)
I'm gonna cook and make this room smell
dangerous! I'll make us outlaws yet!

Blake waves around a few mustard branches in solidarity and
marches in her direction.

                    BLAKE
I'm right behind you Fushay!

Mustard colored dust sprays itself through the air. Alarming.

Beth now alone, yells out..

BETH

If anyone cares, I'm headin' to the barn to
Q.C the scent levels of the next shipment!

Fushay's muffled approval is barely audible.

FADE OUT:

EXT BARN – NIGHT

The moon shines over the barn shingles.

Motion lights CLICK ON. CLICK OFF.

SOUND - COUGH. ...COUGH.

The Barn Door bounces a few times before it wiggles closed.

EXT FARM HOUSE – NIGHT

Blake jogs in his underwear towards the Barn. He whispers loudly
over his shoulder.

BLAKE

Fushay! Beth! Keep up. There's something
in the barn!

Only takes a moment. Fushay and Beth appear at the Farm House
front door. They trail Blake.

EXT BARN DOOR – NIGHT

Blake examines the unlocked Barn Door. The Women stand with distance between them.

                    BETH
          Hmm. That's not good.

SOUND - COUGH.

They look at each other, shrug and head inside. No wilting flowers here.

INT BARN – NIGHT

Fushay flips on the light.

Pollen swims in the air. Fresh cut poppies marked 'SCENTED' line table tops, ready to ship.

Looks like a BOOTLEG operation.

SOUND - COUGH.

                    BLAKE
          Benadryl won't save you Girl!

More - COUGHING.

                    BETH
          Come out before the pollen gets you good!

FUSHAY

Whoever's there. Show yourself!

Out from the shadows come 2 figures.

One Woman (MARILYN) and One Man (RANDAL) in their 60's.

They're wearing very dark shades.

BLAKE

The Stevie Wonder generation.

RANDAL

We're photo-sensitive.

FUSHAY

I'd say you're more than that. Why're you creepin' around our barn?

MARILYN

We're not here to steal anything.

BLAKE

That's a relief. But, let's try it again. Why are you scaring the shit out of us?

RANDAL

The Colony mandates extreme dim lighting policy to save energy. Our eyes have adjusted down but now they won't adjust back up. It's hard to see stuff in these bright lights.

BLAKE

I feel so bad for you. ..(Psych). But again, what does that have to do with you being in our barn?

MARILYN

We're basically nocturnal now.

FUSHAY

Are you two for real?

MARILYN

Sorry to be poking around.

BETH

Again. An apology. And a master deflection. Now, spill it. Why ..are ..you ..here?

Marilyn digs in her jeans pocket, pulls out a rumpled paper.

She reads from it.

MARILYN

We want to know why you left the Colony?

FUSHAY

Why we left the Colony?

RANDAL

Yes.

BETH

I don't understand. Do we know you?

MARILYN

Not personally.

FUSHAY

You're punking us right? This's R&D for a new Blumhouse Horror Series? Right?

BLAKE

Ya, but it won't be good. Cause nothin' is happening, just a lot of talking.

Beth and Fushay nod.

RANDAL

We came here for one simple answer to one simple question.

They wait.

MARILYN

We want to know..

And wait…

MARILYN

..how you could just pick up and leave the Colony for this Outpost?

Silence.

BLAKE

I heard about this on the internet. It's called Hysterical Surrealist Syndrome. It's a manic reaction to societal chaos. It's a totally real thing that took over Earth a millennium ago.

FUSHAY

Is there someone we can call for you?

Randal takes out a piece of paper from his jeans and reads it quite formally.

RANDAL

You! You, young people. We live in an over populated and very loud Colony stricken with poverty, crime, bacteria, and isolation. You forced us into retirement without even a golden handcuff opportunity. We live too long now due to your scientific discoveries and don't have enough money to pay for the extra years. You left us to stare into space, in the solitary confinement of over- priced elderly home condo cubicles that don't allow pets while screaming about your lack of inheritance. Cause we still have mortgages! And then you leave us there, in the Colony. And we want to know why?

BETH
But we don't know you. Do you know us?

BLAKE
Is this a debate over who out - messed -who generationally? Cause for starters, you guys killed the Colony! My future kids will have to live underground just to survive the crazy tornados caused by the volatile weather patterns. The internet porn killed my intimacy barometer so my girlfriend left me. And my grocer tells me cricket powder is the new red meat! But what made my heart die, is my lack of curiosity. A bad habit formed by the Colony search engine which reinforces my base profile algorithm repetitively without deviation. Does this answer your question Sir? The reason we left the Colony is cause of people like you! The reason we live in this Outpost is because of people like her. Fushay. Who gave us back our nose. And my enjoyment for smell and living. Which has all been but snuffed out by fragile allergic people who I feel bad for but not really, cause they are cramping my lot in life with all their damn restrictions! Finally, why on earth, (even

though we're not there) would this make
any big WUPP to you?

Marilyn has heard enough. She pulls out a Molotov Cocktail from thin air.

And a lighter wand magically appears in her hand. (She must be ambidextrous).

It takes everyone a minute to compute the significance of these fast moves.

> BETH
> Before you pitch that flame thrower up on
> our harvest.., which of all the diatribes is
> the most offensive to you? I have to know.

Beth takes a step forward.

> RANDAL
> Hold up.

Beth holds up.

The lighter wand just got LIT!

> MARILYN
> Yes. Y'all, this is happening.

> BLAKE
> I can't believe.. this is happening.

FUSHAY

This can't …be happening. ..Because no one knows why ..this is happening.

RANDAL

I don't think it matters. Cause it's too complicated! Just focus on avoiding the burning and explosions.

Beat.

BLAKE

Again, I feel like there's too many topics streaming all at once to make sense of everything. I think we need a talking stick.

FUSHAY

Hey. I'll summarize the speeches. (Since nothing else is going on). Basically. You old people are mad cause we left the Colony. We left the Colony cause we want to smell stuff in the Outpost. And the law says those that are allergic to smells have the right —a- way, like pedestrians in a bike lane. But explain this to me. What's your connection to all that and why does burnin' our harvest solve the Colony problems you describe?

RANDAL

It doesn't. This is a scorched earth mission.

(Even though we're not there). The just of
it is, If I can't be happy, neither can you.

FUSHAY

Well, that is an attention getter.

BETH

It's an attention getter but nothin' really
changes. I don't get it.

BLAKE

So, really this is revenge. Served Cold. You
don't even know us. So, this is random. So
colder than cold. Conclusion, To burn our
harvest will make you feel good. That's it
then. The bottom line to it all.

MARILYN

Yes, It's a road rage kind of event.
Random. Unconnected. But meaningful to
me. That's correct.

They all just stand there. Thinking and contemplating. ...

Marilyn throws the Molotov down.

The flowers fry up – fast, hot and smelly.

Heavy smoke ignites the pollen to a deadly mixture. It curls up
brown into the air.

COUGHING. Lots of COUGHING.

Everyone runs out and sprawls onto the lawn.

EXT BARN – NIGHT

The Motion Detector lights flick ON and OFF.

EXT BARN LAWN - NIGHT

Blake holds a shovel over Randal.

They both watch the arson blaze on. Nothing else moves.

> BLAKE
> You blew up our harvest!

> BETH
> Technically he didn't. Hold up!

Marilyn is COUGHING uncontrollably. She's a mess.

> FUSHAY
> What do we do with 'em?

> BETH
> What do you suggest? We're in the boondocks.

> BLAKE

Yes. We are.

FUSHAY

Blake. Put down the shovel. Damn.

BLAKE

Oh, I'm snapped! I want to feel good too! I want revenge on a plate too! This situation is, 'Done like Dinner'.

Blake screams and beats Randal to stillness with the shovel.

The Women stand there. And watch.

BLAKE

Oops. I guess I didn't pass the marshmallow test.

MARILYN

Marshmallow?

BLAKE

How long you can resist a bowl of marshmallows when told not to eat them.

MARILYN

I don't know.

BLAKE

No, that's the impulse control test. You're not supposed to eat them.

Marilyn looks blank.

                    BLAKE
        Ever. You are to resist the marshmallow.
        Like the Borg. Resist… Damn it!

                    MARILYN
        Oh. You ate them.

                    BLAKE
        Exactly. But you did too.

                    MARILYN
        Yes, I did. Toasted on a stick.

                    BLAKE
        Very Toasty. Yes.

                    FUSHAY
        She lit our barn on fire! She threatened us
        in the middle of the night! (Which is very
        disorienting). The Colony's gonna be
        sooooo pissed! If we talked to them I
        mean. They would be…pissed.

Suddenly, Marilyn makes a sloppy run to the Farm House.

Beth, Blake and Fushay are stunned.

Then they sprint after her.

EXT FARM HOUSE PORCH – NIGHT

Marilyn hits the porch in good stride.

She flies through the screen door while the rest give chase a ways behind.

INT FARM HOUSE – NIGHT

Once inside, using her lighter wand, Marilyn lights any fabric she can get close to. Curtains are a favorite.

She moves fast through the house, still wearing her shades.

Beth, Fushay and Blake lead a disorganized chase through the house. But Marilyn easily eludes them.

Beth then flanks off, to put out a fire start that has caught a pail of dried mustard weeds.

The air is hot. The flames light the room yellow. The smoke dusts dull her once sharp sights.

> FUSHAY
>
> I can't see!

> BETH
>
> Do your best!

> BLAKE
>
> I think I found her!

FLAILING. GROPING. COUGHING. RED FLAMES. BROWN
SMOKE. YELLOW DUST.

EXT FARM HOUSE – NIGHT

Marilyn stands outside the burning house watching flames grab
stars.

She re-positions her shades on her nose.

She is stoic to the CRIES for HELP coming from the house.

She sits down. Settles in. The night is less dark now and the fire less
hot.

EXT SUNRISE OVER POPPY FIELDS - DAYBREAK

It's quiet but for a slight wind. Red poppies roll out in large
swatches like yoga mats on a desert colored wooden floor.

SOUND – a deep inhale through the nose.

> MARILYN (O.S)
> Smell the mood on that!

THE END.

THE QUEEN COLONIES

Annelise Knoot

Lasi remembered the touch of sun. Once. She and Nigel had climbed to the surface, scavenging for scraps, chunks of cement pried loose could be used for supports where the columns spiralled down for miles in the core's womb, throbbing life into humanity even as acidic rain ate its surface.

Lasi had wandered to the lake's mouldy edge, Nigel close behind, and stared at the pitted lumps of empty island. Sitting on the twisted steel wreckage of some kind of amphitheatre, a crack had broken in the cement clouds. The light touched her, streaked right across her face for a moment and she felt what could only be described as summertime. Nigel had cried out, his small world turned bloody beneath tight shut lids. His first time seeing the burst of scarlet that was his own blood.

All night, they whispered about it, brother and sister clutching hands in the empty bedroom before going to sleep.

Lasi, alone, picked up a chunk of cement and whipped it into the lake. It lodged with a resounding squelch. She glanced up, but no one approached. Only a few bodies skittered around, searching the stones with mineral and organic sensors, broke up the pallid ruins of Old Toronto. None stared at the sky.

Her father would say it a good thing. Not to trust the colony recruiters that demanded life be lived amongst the stars. Until he won the lottery and left too. Colonized.

Lasi's life ended shortly after that day. Not in the physical sense. Lasi stood, staring at her dusty gloves. Clearly, she was still here. But Nigel was not.

She had walked through the tunnels to pick up rations, one pack of mags (nicer name than maggots) each. Hungry eyes watched her return, salivating on their own shares, but it was never enough to fill a body. She and Nigel had eaten, played rock, paper, scissors, and went to bed, listening to the whisper of air vents push oxygen up from the core. In the morning her brother was gone. They had even left a note. "You can't work, you can't eat." It didn't matter that he had scavenged with her. He was small and an easy excuse for Hunger. Someone would take him, take his ration, and drop him. She never saw Nigel again.

Lasi left the queasy remains and joined the trickle of scavengers back to the entrance, her rucksack bulging with chunks of cement, 2 credits apiece. No one manned the gap in the wall, the staircase of metal slats leading down to pitch black. Why would they? No one wanted to be out, only further down.

Lasi flowed with the stream, sluggish, listening to the hum of talk. She felt cold. Colder than usual.

Blue and green light shone ahead, the cheery neon signs flickering in and out of life in the dark. It must be a good sign, that they could afford the electricity. Lasi contemplated the nearest, blue sand beaches, purple trees and a bikini clad woman running through. SAND CASTLE COLONY, burned under her, the words in such impossible white that they left an imprint on her retinas, another form of advertisement. Perhaps they did send you somewhere good and her father had been wrong to be paranoid.

Lasi broke off from the trek on the first set of halls opening into the ground, leaving the main path of descent to the warm depths of the core. Her halls were flecked in bio-illumination. Mushrooms too small to be eaten and helpfully poisonous glowed along the ceiling, cultivated by her tunnel neighbours. She brushed her fingers along the wall, feeling the bone aching chill of stone advance through her glove.

Her parents' house waited at the end. Sub-Level 1. All they could ever afford. Lasi banged the door open, feeling her ownership in the etched 'N' scratched across the metal's face.

Inside the only light came from the potted luminescent 'shrooms. Lasi crossed and deposited her rucksack on the floor. It thumped, the garbled collection of broken concrete scattering. A door creaked and Lasi glanced over, not that she could make out his form in the shadows.

A few lodgers had come and gone over the three years since Nigel vanished. Lasi had made her parents' room her home and she couldn't stand to have that other door shut on aching emptiness.

Melanoce moved in. A pale, empty shell of a being. He never spoke. Never turned on the lights. It saved on the hydro bill.

She could hear his feet skitter down the hall to his room, avoiding her as usual. Lasi sighed and followed his echo down the hall, eager to sink in the softness of her fungus mattress, stuffed freshly last week, and sleep the day away.

A dull patter sounded overhead, flecks of rain dancing across the ceiling. She hoped it would not flood. Sleeping in the cold and the damp hardly appealed and the rain sometimes glowed disconcerting colours, stained with pollutants and reacting with the bioluminescence in the walls.

Lasi yanked the blankets over her head and turned into her pillow. She remembered the sun again, that flash of light, the bloody imprint of her lids. Who knew closing your eyes could be so bright? She wanted that heat now, that shock of life to rattle her again.

The floorboards creaked outside, and she flipped over staring at the bleary outline of her door orbited by the tiny caps of blue mushrooms. The one annoying tick of Melanoce. He lurked in her periphery when it rained. She could picture the shift of his weight, bound in hesitation outside her door. What was it tonight? Did the room leak? Is that why he couldn't mind his own business? But he never knocked. She wasn't even sure if he knew how aware she was of him, waiting, wondering.

Lasi sat up in bed and the creaking stilled. She shivered, pulling the wrap of her blanket closer, made of plastic, shining silver. The same blankets used in the spaceships that travelled to the colonies.

She tiptoed across the room and pressed a hand to the door, feeling the stick of her flesh against the metal. Tonight she could break the cold. Lasi pulled the door open and there he was, pale hair slick across his scalp, nose turned up in a point in contrast to his downcast eyes.

Reaching out, Lasi caught his sleeve and tugged. He took a step forward, crossing the unspoken boundary of three months. Every rain, he had offered and finally she needed him.

Lasi led him to the bed and they sat, not touching, not even looking at each other. She could hear his breath, quick and fast through his mouth and eventually, a pale hand slipped into her own.

When she woke the next morning she felt good. Unexpectedly so. She could not remember the last time her blood had coursed, had felt the pounding of her heart in her ears, had realized that skin could still feel. She had forgotten she could still want.

She rolled over expecting the bed to be empty, but he was there, perched on its edge, his shoulders rising and falling in sleep. She pressed a kiss to his bare skin and left to hunt the surface again. The rain had ended. Real life returned.

•

Infestations were common underground. Two animal species had notably escaped the deluge of poison sky, the blast that had shattered so much stone: cockroaches and ants. Lasi squinted, her flashlight sputtering out even as she registered the small black bodies moving in tandem across the kitchen floor. Everyone had known the cockroaches would be a problem, even before the destruction's occurrence. The old days mentioned their power and survivability, a thing to be abhorred and admired. But no one had expected the ants.

Silly really, Lasi thought sitting back on her heels to crank the flashlight into service. The handle whizzed. Ants lived below ground before humans. People complained about them, saying they followed humanity into the terratropolises in search of food, stealing away organics and digging tunnels through their own, cradling crumbs to their queens. As far as Lasi was concerned, the ants were here first, but she still didn't want them in her house.

Ant killer, Lasi decided. Flicking the beam back on their trail. She had a few cupboards housing lumps of grainy bread bought with precious credits from the core. She could not risk the ants revealing their location to those who wandered in the dark.

Lasi let the door bang behind her and walked carefully through her hall, rapping once on her neighbour's door to let the old woman know she was going out. A courtesy and a defence for their little tunnel community.

She joined the path of workers, some trudging up, elbows brushing hers, their eyes fixed on the glimmer of hope that the surface would provide a new bounty. Down to sub-level 7, the surfacer market. She brushed through the milling people, voices louder here, more comfortable, safe from leaking poisons and acid rain. People laughed, people cried, people shouted. Too may people. Lasi shouldered around a collection of men guffawing at a woman whose dress plummeted between her breasts and lumi-paint accented her curves. Tunnel walkers, another way to make a living, but hardly a safe one. Lasi shook her head and continued through the press of hungry bodies.

No one knew what was in the water from the wells but somehow it had affected fertility. People were birthing three, maybe four babes at a time. So many mouths did not bode well for a society rationed to maggots, living in close quarters, burying into the earth. They could only go so far. You could not dig straight to the core.

Another reason Nigel vanished. He was a child and children have lost their value. Lasi pondered, staring at the open market stall, picking up a slim cannister of ant killer, some ridiculously overpriced from the core, others in old liquor bottles, homemade in the first seven levels. She chose one, squeezing the glass between her fingers and staring at the other items, feeling like she had forgotten something. Lasi's eyes flitted over sensor rods, boxes of tape, bottles of glue, fabrics rested from the core, a woolen blanket. Lasi passed her hand over it, not daring to touch.

"Real wool?" She asked, catching the shop keep's eye.

He nodded and beamed. "Cost me an arm and a leg but she's the real deal. I'm looking for a half million credits for it."

Lasi removed her hand, the belief of its warmth enough to warrant such an outlandish price.

"I think I'll just take this." She followed him under the canvas. It rattled under the pelt of cascading dirt.

The shop keep popped open a tin, revealing a small electronic card reader to take her credits. She began counting the sum of the last sale, wondering how much of a dent he would try and levy her way.

Just behind him stood a stack of men's and women's hygiene items and Lasi's counting scattered. She had not been keeping track, had no reason to, living as a scavenger, sleeping alone. Mostly. She wasn't on medication like a tunnel walker. She had felt so achingly empty, she had not thought she could carry anything more than scrap.

Lasi passed the man her card with shaking hands. The quick swipe, beep of acceptance and she was back in the crowd, feeling like someone had cast a spotlight on her. Two months. The last time she had scavenged by the lake and Melanoce…

She darted back into the stairwell and ran further down, chewing her lip until the flesh began to shred. Sub level 13 was a cacophony of glittering signs, the first installation of elevators leading into Sub-Toronto's depths. Lasi ignored the sparkle, the whirring of gears as boxes descended to richer realms.

She walked to the little black tent, tucked away from the gleam of billboards advertising prices for lunar mansions, the dates for the next colony launch, a picture of a giant winged woman, her crown glowing bright gold proclaiming the Queen Colony in full operation.

She double checked to make sure no one saw her enter. The location was not well known, the outside unmarked except for those told. Her neighbour had mentioned it. A woman's clinic.

No one greeted her inside. Empty but for another opaque sheet, fluttering from the passage of people behind it.

"Hello?" Lasi called and the movement stilled.

"Come to the curtain." A woman's voice answered.

Lasi approached, her gut cramping.

The rest of the affair flew by, quick and curtained. She never saw the woman's face, both their identities remained in obscurity. Too many people did not want to know about children, about the choices made for them. But the vial of blue could not lie. She was pregnant.

Lasi dragged her feet through the square, wandering in the light of sub level 13 as she considered her options. She could stay and hide the children. There would be more than one, always was. But hiding them… squealing babies with flapping mouths, the influx of rations to her sub level 1 doorway. That could turn her own neighbours on her, destroy their sense of security, just like the glass shattering when Nigel vanished. She could not keep them there.

The government then. They took all children offered. Down in the lower levels, maybe she could visit. Offer them up for test subjects, their pink skin falling to the pinprick of needles. They would have a life of sorts. Like Melanoce. He had listed a government office on his rental application as his birth place.

Lasi glanced around, trying to place herself in the flickering light and trudged back to the main staircase.

She burst through the door and caught Melanoce at the kitchen counter, his ration of mags on the table still wriggled feebly. He flinched when she approached, staring at the ground.

"I'm pregnant." The words hissed out like a gas leak, an invisible threat ticking down the seconds of her life.

Melanoce met her gaze for a split second, unresponsive.

"I won't tell." Quiet, faint, the brush of a moth's wing on her face. Lasi trembled at the sound of his voice, wanting to latch onto its timbre and form a shield of quiet sound around the pulse pounding in her ears.

Too many cracks in the walls. Too close to the surface for secrets. She shook her head and whispered, "Maybe the government?"

The flicker of familiarity between them died and Melanoce flattened in his seat. Shrunken, stoic, he shook his head once.

Lasi watched him walk past her and into her brother's bedroom without another sign that she existed in his life.

Abortion could be an option. Lasi paced the kitchen, one hand brushing over her stomach, wondering if she could feel a bulge. Irritated, she flicked her fingers away and banged out the front door, back into the stream. It couldn't be too late.

She stared at the building for a long time. Lights twinkled from below, illuminating the painted stork, flying free and away, right into the dirt ceiling. Lasi twisted her hands, glancing around every time someone passed. She tried not to look too interested in the building.

A woman caught her eye. Could she know? The woman smiled, her face gently lined, twin braids popping out the front of her head like antennae. She reached out and Lasi twitched, but the woman only offered a pamphlet.

Lasi took it and the woman wandered off without another word, pamphlets tucked under her arm. She stared at the brochure, tilting its surface to catch the leaking light. The same beautified woman with white wings soaring into a night sky. She had seen it in the square, the name sounded familiar. Queen Colony. Another space cast off, trying to rid the earth of her presence, of her portions and her right to walk the city tunnels.

Unfolding the glossy pages, Lasi flitted through the scattered words, bubbled together for easy digestion. Queen Colony, searching for mothers, for fertile women, want a future for you and your kin? Join the Queen Colony today and embrace a life in the stars. An address was printed below in gold letters: Sub Level 60.

Lasi goggled at the number. What did sub level 60 have to offer someone so close to the surface? The core never bothered with surface scum. Her kind were scraped off by lotteries, colonies asking for hard labour, or the pretense of a dream-like scam existence, far too happy to pay for you to leave the earth behind.

Searching for mothers… The difference lit a cautious hope. She wouldn't go, it was a suicide mission, but… Lasi glanced at the deadpan stork, its rotting wooden wings. It would provide a distraction, at least. Give her time to make the decision.

Lasi jogged to the main hall and eyed the staircase, all the way down fifty floors. An elevator jangled nearby, the beep of credits poured into its belly as people paid for passage below. Lasi, bit her lip and decided. She leapt for the elevator, squeezing through just as the doors shut without any loss of her precious credits.

The assembled men and women complained, shoving her back against the now locked grate, but eventually subsisted under the roar of compressed air as they rocketed down: destination sub level 60.

Lasi felt confident she could run before anyone raised real complaint. The elevator slowed and Lasi felt her eyes begin to burn.

Light blinded. Every wall lined with gold bulbs, pouring out amber warmth and a clarity that reminded her of the sun. She blinked, tears streaming and threw herself through the doors. Running through blindness, she could not even take in the beauty of the core's atrium.

The flyer led her through exquisite architecture. Tunnels carved out of the rock from caring hands, not shunted into existence by desperate pickaxe, the fear of destruction goading them on.

The centre's white doors waited at the end of the third hall, gleaming with frosted glass. They slid open on a sensor as she approached and Lasi felt stymied by the excessive use of electricity.

"Hello, miss." A woman with a sharp black bob and jutting lips watched her from behind the pristine desk. "My name is Myr Mecia. Are you interested in the Queen Colony?"

Lasi glanced at the flyer in her hand and twisted the lacquered pages between her fingers. "I suppose. Interested why you're asking for fertile women, anyway." Lasi shrugged and shuffled forward.

Myr Mecia beamed at Lasi and flipped open a binder filled with prints of a glossy blue planet, hovering in space and surrounded by clouds. It rang a bell in Lasi's memory, some resource planet they had colonized a few decades ago.

"That's that honeydew planet, right?" Lasi finally asked after Myr Mecia made no attempt to explain the images.

"Correct."

Lasi shifted uncomfortably. Myr Mecia did not give any further sign that she wanted to share information about the colony.

"So," Lasi finally said, hands shoved in her pockets. "What's this about?"

Myr Mecia flashed that smile again, her teeth hardly showing through her overly pouted lips, like mandibles protruding from her face.

"The Queen Colony is looking to recruit fertile women to send to the colony on Honeydew. Are you interested in signing up?" She produced a clipboard from the bowels of her desk and laid it in front of Lasi, a pen uncapped and waiting chained to its side.

"No, well, why should I be? What does it offer?"

"We provide women with lodgings in the core until departure, scheduled every three months to the Queen Colony. We require that women conceive a child and take it with them on their journey, in utero of course, to give birth on the planet."

"Why?" Lasi asked, the concept so obviously fraught she could hardly believe the woman presented it.

Myr Mecia's smile dropped and she sighed. "The journey requires passage through a wormhole. And that passage has been found to sterilize those travelling. Unless those people are born on the planet. We need the honeydew the planet supplies. As you may know, it's an imperative fuel to maintain the ecospheres on the lunar mansions, which is why this luxurious proposal is being made to women of all levels."

Myr Mecia sounded a bit too knowing and Lasi brushed at the hem of her shirt, coated in grey dust.

"We will take anyone under the understanding they will be inseminated and sent to the colony. Once there they will deliver a baby who will stay and live on the colony. The woman then has a choice to return to earth, like all colonists, or stay and make a new life there."

It was exactly what Lasi had been waiting for and she pounced. "Like all colonists. None of them ever return."

Myr Mecia raised her eyebrow. "I did."

"What?"

"I returned from the colony." Myr Mecia shrugged, as if this knowledge were commonplace. "I went for touring purposes and had no reason to stay. The company offered me a great package to come back and work in a terratropolis for recruitment. My family's from Sub-Toronto."

Lasi felt shaken. The woman was not selling the colony at all how the billboards or lottery did. She did not seem to care whether

Lasi signed up or not.

"Look," Myr Mecia said, punctuating Lasi's thoughts. "Colonies have their dangers. No one offering a legitimate ride would tell you otherwise. Things go wrong in space travel, diseases appear on alien planets we're not ready to deal with. But the Queen Colony is different. It's well established, has four surface cities and a booming economy. People are killing to get a ticket to go there rather than the labour colonies and honestly if you're not interested, then you should go."

Lasi wavered, the possibility of successful colonies existing shocked her. She had really thought the government sent them up there just to be rid of them. "What about the lotteries? Do those colonies exist? My father…" Lasi trailed off, not sure what she wanted to hear.

"I can only speak to what I've seen." Myr Mecia said. "Honeydew exists. It's fuel for the mansions so they exist too. You see them, when you break through the atmosphere." Her gaze softened and she grinned. "That's where I'd like to end up, in the long run. Beautiful view of the moon and the sun," She shivered and brushed a hand against her bob. "I've never experienced light like that anywhere else."

"I'll sign."

Lasi scribbled her name on the form, the image of sunlight blinding her as thoroughly as neon. She followed Myr Mecia into the centre.

"Now, all women who sign are guaranteed the six months in the core. Only those who conceive are sent to the colony. Your insemination date will be discussed." Myr Mecia opened a door.

Lasi's mouth hung open. A glittering crystal heart reflected firelight into a sparkling display around the polished stone walls.

Water pounded at the crystal's base, a fountain encircling its origin. Everything shone and sparkled. Lasi could even hear music playing, electronic and sharp, through hidden speakers somewhere.

"We offer a suite here at the centre, I can get you set up. Once you are inseminated we ask that you do not return to the surface as there are dangers to pregnant women above. You will be safe in the centre and anywhere else in the core which you can access through the crystal."

Myr Mecia gestured to the sparkling spire. Lasi noticed a small pod rising through the crystal's core to ding on the level just below her feet.

"Would you like to be shown your room? Do you have anyone you need to speak with first on your level? Forgive my saying so, but you look like a surfacer."

Lasi thought of Melanoce, skulking back to his room with stiff shoulders, unable to bear the responsibility of their act and shook her head. "No one. I'll stay. But, I'm already pregnant."

Myr Mecia's eyebrows rose and she pulled the fat binder out from under her arm. "I see." She flipped through laminated pages, leaning on the silver banister.

Lasi stared at the crystal. The tip fractured sparkling light over the rock ceiling. It picked up flecks of gold and green and Lasi wondered if they were gem stones embedded. She had heard rumours of the lower levels treating the precious stones as no more than décor, but to see it was another thing.

"Alright then." Myr Mecia snapped the binder shut and led Lasi down a pristine hallway.

"Does that change something?" Lasi asked, anxiety ricocheting as the surroundings became increasingly familiar, if still brighter than she was used to.

"Only the duration of your stay." Myr Mecia stopped in front of a door and entered the room.

A sparkling clean examination table took up most of the floor space. A blocky computer monitor glowed white in the corner.

"Up on the table, please." Myr Mecia pressed a button on the wall and Lasi heard the faint sound of a buzzer. "We need to check how far along you are. If the fetuses are too matured, they cannot pass through the wormhole without suffering complications."

Lasi nodded, apprehensive and waited on the table. Myr Mecia left the room and a man entered, wearing a white robe of real cotton. Lasi stared at the cloth in amazement, wanting to feel its softness in her fingers.

The man did not bother to introduce himself but set to warming up the machine. He took her vitals, recorded them on a clipboard then asked her to lift her shirt and rubbed her belly down with cold, clinging jelly. He next passed a sensor across her stomach, nodding to himself, listening to the whir. Then he nodded again and left the room.

Lasi sat up and rubbed the slime off her stomach, wondering what her father would say. She shook her head. He would say this was insane. A crazy idea brought on by panic, not logic.

Myr Mecia bustled back in through the door. "You still have time."

"How much?" Lasi asked, skittering off the table. A headache was beginning to pound between her temples, her eyes tired from the light.

"A month before you would have been past our cut off."

Lasi sighed with relief.

"But, to stay qualified our next scheduled departure is at the end of the week."

Lasi shook her head. "So I can take the next one, in a month."

Myr Mecia raised an eyebrow. "There won't be one. We fly every three months on our schedule, as I said. You either take the one at the end of the week or you're not going."

Lasi curled her fingers around her biceps, staring at the flickering computer monitor. The screen hosted a black and white image, curling lines, three blobs. She stared without seeing.

"I need to think about this."

"You already signed."

"So I'll unsign. I just need to think." Lasi snapped, pushing past the clean-cut woman and back into the hall.

Lasi walked quickly, ignoring the flecks of jewelled glitter tempting her eye. She shoved out the doors, smacking into their sides before they could fully open and ran through the illumination, seeking shadows.

•

Rain pattered overhead, bouncing off the steel wreckage of a decayed shopping mall. She stared at the empty ruins wondering if there even was a right choice. She could keep scavenging, bringing back chunks of cement. Gather her savings until she had enough credit to buy a place on level 3, just low enough to be away from the rain, but not so close to the market to be loud. Melanoce could come too.

Thinking of him, she pressed a hand to her stomach and remembered his touch, the quiet existence together, the heat of her bedroom. Lasi wondered if he had ever lost anyone. Growing up as lab rat in the government facility, who would he have known? Would she leave him behind the way her father had left? Maybe a cursory email back about life on a new planet, that he should sign up too. Maybe not even written by her hand, but just someone else trying to destroy the excess of hungry mouths.

Lasi padded back into the dark, her rucksack full of cement. The stream of scavengers was slighter, the threat of rain heavy in the air, though according to Myr Mecia it would not fall till the week's end, the scheduled date of the launch.

She thrust her door open and walked in. The kitchen stood empty. The glow of mushrooms pathetic compared to the crystal glimmer of the core.

"Melanoce?" She called softly, half hoping he would not respond. She could leave a letter maybe.

But the door to her brother's old bedroom creaked and his ashen form shuffled out, watching her. A shadow in the shadows.

"I'm," Lasi started, but the words caved in her throat.

She set the rucksack down and her key to the apartment. Lasi hesitated and pushed the key across the table to the glowing mushrooms, in case he could not see it in the gloom.

"Goodbye."

She crossed quickly to the door and he followed, feet shuffling. She swung around to stare at him and he reached out, catching and cradling her stomach between his hands. His skin warmed her through the thin stretch of shirt. She could not see his face in the dark, but could feel his gaze wandering over her face as it never did in the light. Lips pressed to hers, light and brief.

After a minute, he lowered his hands. Lasi took a step back and the door thudded shut between them.

~

Myr Mecia walked her through the protocols of the flight.

"Normally, a tech runner would do this, but I want to ensure you understand everything clearly." Myr Mecia had to shout over the rumble of sound in the airy chamber as the narrow grey pods started up, growling. Women chattered all around, clambering into their pods, assisted by tech runners and doctors. Three hundred in the flight, twenty more than last time she had heard and another two hundred already signed up for the next flight in another three months.

Lasi shivered as she followed, a clamminess eating through her gut.

"These are the *Alates*." Myr Mecia gestured at the narrow, single person pods. "They have been equipped with the medical equipment necessary for your health and the health of your fetuses in space. You will be strapped in, but conscious for the duration of the trip. It's a bit icky," Myr Mecia said, pointing inside at the rows of tubes running like feelers through the *Alate's* interior. "You will be very much plugged in from every conceivable orifice, but it's for your safety and theirs." She nodded at Lasi's stomach.

"I thought we'd be in cryo." Lasi commented, trying not to imagine the tubes fastening to her flesh.

A woman nearby laughed at her question and said, "That would damage the babies." She waved a sonogram at Lasi's face. Black, white, and rubbery, Lasi turned away. Another woman caught her eye, gaze empty. Lasi felt she knew her. She too, had no other way out.

"Yes." Myr Mecia nodded and pushed Lasi on. "The journey only lasts seventy-two hours as it is. The worm hole cuts down on the total distance." Myr Mecia paused in front of an empty *Alate*. "Climb on in, Lasi."

Lasi stared and felt her mouth pop open, searching for a question to delay her sequestering. "Why can't we all travel together? Wouldn't one big ship be more efficient?"

Myr Mecia shook her head, checking her watch. "They can't go through the worm hole. It limits more than you would think but it's damned convenient otherwise. A hundred years to get to that planet the long way and time is not on our side. We need the honeydew. We need this colony to be successful."

"I don't want to go." Lasi said suddenly and turned on her heel, ready to stride off the scene and back into her shadowed life.

Myr Mecia grabbed her arm. "Lasi, I'm sorry."

Lasi hesitated, thoughts pinging around faster than a subterranean elevator.

"I know this is going quickly and its scary to think about space." The words came out in a gush. The hangar doors were opening. "But you should make sure you're certain, before getting in there." Myr Mecia rustled in the pocket of her jacket. "Maybe this will help."

She passed Lasi a folded picture, black, white and wiggly. Three tiny beans stacked one on top of the other. "These are mine?" Lasi asked staring at the picture.

"Yours."

Her little beans lifting shadow fingers to wave at her.

"Alright."

Myr Mecia shuffled her into the pod and vanished. Suddenly a tech runner was on her and tubes suctioned into her skin, beeping filled her ears, ricocheting out as it registered her heart beat. She stared at the photo the entire time, counting and recounting the figures. *One. Two. Three.*

"Ready and set. Good luck on the other side, miss." The tech runner said, hopping back out of the pod.

Lasi stared back at him uncomprehending. She reached to feel the tube of oxygen hanging under her nose and around her ears.

He pressed a button and the capsule door descended, sealing shut with a satisfying click. A small circular window looked out on the scene as fumes began to fill the room. Lasi shuffled in her seat feeling the pull of tubes between her legs and on her wrists. She tried to remain still, nausea rising in her stomach.

A countdown boomed through speakers somewhere in the hangar. 3. *One,* Lasi thought. 2. *Two.* 1. *Three.*

The *Alate* wriggled, jostling her against the padded harness holding her in place, and blasted from the ground. Lasi's teeth shook in her skull as the pod trembled into the air. Through the window she could see the grey light of day break across the other pods as they ricocheted up. They were flying.

Flecks of rain spattered the pod window when they broke cover, trickling past and obscuring her vision of the other pods' vapor trails spiralling over the grey earth. She squeezed the sonogram between her fingers.

Earth fell away, blurry and distant. The swarm of *Alates* slid through the uppermost layer of clouds. Lasi cringed away from her window. A flicker of lightning sparked in the cloudy vapours outside. Wriggles of multicoloured light flew across the window and vanished from Lasi's sight.

As the *Alates* broke through the uppermost layer of clouds, light emerged. Sunshine, bright and yellow blared from the far side of her pod, reflecting off an adjacent pod and blinding her. Lasi squinted hard, soaking in the first brush against real sunshine. For a moment, the woman in the nearby pod was illuminated, her face pressed against the window in awe. A tremulous smile brushed Lasi's lips and the pod burst.

Lasi jerked back with a yell as flame engulfed the other woman. The heart monitor beeped wildly, filling her ears with her own panic. The Alate fell back to the swirling grey mist surrounding the planet, no hope of saving itself.

Lasi whimpered and pressed back in her seat, clutching the photo against her chest. The pod curved again, its back still to the sunlight and Lasi stared reluctantly down at the shrinking planet. The fiery trails of two other pods falling like fain back to the dead earth. The *Alate* curled around again. Ahead stretched a mass of tangled satellite steel.

"Please, no!" Lasi shrieked, pounding her fists on the pod's wall. "Go around, go up, go up!"

The pod did not respond, automated to its own path. It drifted lazily, curling to the wreckage. The scream of metal vying with metal curdled in Lasi's stomach and she thought it was the end. A flicker of sparks out the window. She took a deep breath preparing for the fire, but the pod passed through.

A boom and blast of fiery air washed over. Some other pod. Not as lucky. Her *Alate* pirouetted and she looked back again. Three pods followed to the satellite graveyard. Two hit with force so hard they popped, accelerating the mass of metal after her own pod. Another *Alate* veered into view and a twisted rod caught its window. Lasi saw the spurt of blood, crimson, lit by sunshine before that pod, too, caught flame.

The hunk of satellite bore down, chasing, but her *Alate* seemed to have decided it was in a hurry. With a burst of speed, the pod and its passenger pulsed through space, leaving the dying hunks behind.

Lasi shuddered in her seat, each sounding harsh in her own ears, the only organic sound available. The darkness engulfed her. Any cabin lights flickered away into the periphery as she stared out.

Infinite space, empty but for the pinpricks of light, stars faint ahead. She felt like she was in the tunnels again, gazing at the soft glow of mushrooms and she wondered if Melanoce had watched her pod fly away.

The Alate turned again and light spilled inside. Lasi stared down at her pink fingers, scrubbed clean of the clinging grey dust, her white space suit dotted with wires, the half imagined swell of her belly. Leaning forward she closed her eyes and red dominated her vision. As the Alate curled again, the light shifting from view, she pressed the sonogram to the window, showing them the sun and stared at the picture in the light of day. Lasi counted their heads.

One, two, three.

•

Every summer, ant species send out thousands upon thousands of flying ants to create new colonies, all "in the hopes that just one or two of them might succeed" (Antkeepers, 2018).[1]

---

1 Antkeepers. (2018). Flying Ants and the Impressive Nuptial Flights – Antkeepers. [online] Available at: https://www.antkeepers.com/facts/ants/flying-ants/ [Accessed 1 Oct. 2018].

AN AGE OF CHANGES

Patrick Darvis

Year 5 of the Age of Worlds-Crossing (592 by human calendar)

"Where is it? Where is the Outpost" asked Caldarian as he emerged from the entrance of the cave in which stood the Rift between worlds.

"This way," replied his mother. "At the bottom of the valley."

Looking down the slope, the elf child saw a wall circling a large cluster of tents.

When they neared the gate several hours later, Caldarian looked up at the elf warriors wearing the sea-green colored armors of Islelder custom as they stood guard on the wall. His face broke into a joyful grin as he recognized one of them.

"Father is here!" he shouted, pointing him out to his mother.

"Yes, he is," she replied. "But we will have to wait until dusk to meet with him."

"Why dusk?" asked Caldarian in a voice barely hiding his disappointment.

"Because that is when the goblins will replace him to watch over the wall for the night."

Once they had crossed the opening, the newly arrived elves found themselves facing two buildings joined by a gallery with large glass windows. One building was made of white marble in the custom style of the elves, with slender spires and graceful curves. The other was made of grey stone and was shorter and less slender than the Islelder building but was just as large.

"Why are the buildings joined that way?" asked Caldarian.

"So that the humans coming to visit us know that the goblins and elves are equals, and that they have to treat with both our races," replied an elf guide who came to greet the group of elves. "Your tents are this way. Please form a line. When you are called, please state the name of the person you came on Earth to join."

Once it was Caldarian and his mother's turn, they came forward.

"My husband's name is Alathanir," she said. "He is the captain of the guards."

"That would be tent number thirty-six," he said while pointing at the tents near the wall.

One hour later, a bell rang to announce dinner at the dining hall. When he entered the building, Caldarian saw his father and rushed to hug him.

"I see that I have been missed," said Alathanir with a smile.

Accompanied by his parents, the elf child sat at a table. However, his joy at seeing his family reunited again vanished when the food arrived.

"What is this?" he asked, gazing at the coarse bread and the bowl of sloppy soup in front of him.

"This is human food," replied his father. "You will have to get used to it if you want to live on Earth."

"First, we have to live in tents," said Caldarian with a frown, "now we have to eat this stinking food."

"This is Earth. We have to do as the humans do if we want them to accept us. They are making efforts to comply to our customs in order to be allowed access to the Homeworld. We must do the same on Earth if we want to establish good relations. As for the tents, it is just a matter of weeks. With our workers working during the days and the goblins working during the nights, the houses will soon be completed."

Year 10 of the Age of Worlds-Crossing (597 by human calendar)

Breathing softly, Caldarian released the arrow which flew across the training yard and struck the target not far from its center.

"Not bad," said the instructor. "For someone who is barely fifty, you have talent. Your father taught you well."

Once the archery lesson was over, Caldarian grabbed a glass of water. Taking a stroll around the training area, he saw a group of humans enter the Outpost.

Despite himself, he couldn't help but stare at them, finding it unsettling how they were at the same time so similar to the elves while also so different, with their faces being rounder and their builds less slender. In a way, their appearance was stranger and harder to accept than the goblins' grey skin and bat-like triangular noses. Having a bit of free time ahead of him and feeling more curious than disturbed by the humans after having seen them for years, he came closer to see what they were bringing with them.

As usual, it consisted of the strange animals they called birds and sheep. Those who appeared to be their leaders went to the Hall of the Homeworlders. A few minutes later, Caldarian could see them sit at a table in the central gallery, negotiating with the Islelder and goblin ambassadors.

After an hour, an elf approached the humans outside to give them the bat and shark-shaped brooches that would prove they had received authorization to settle on the Homeworld. When they had left the Outpost to head for the Rift leading to the Homeworld,

Caldarian walked home.

Year 395 of the Age of Worlds-Crossing (982 by human calendar)

As a hawk flew across the sky, Caldarian gazed at the valley around him, bow in hand. The sun had started its descent but it would still be one hour before the goblin guards would come to replace their elven counterparts.

"Are my soldiers hungry?" asked a voice behind him.

"Mother, I am on duty," he replied. "I should not be talking to anyone. Father would not approve."

"If he disapproved of such behavior, then we would not have met and you would not exist."

"I confirm," said Alathanir.

Repressing a smile, Caldarian turned his attention back to the road leading to the Outpost and noticed movement.

"Father," he said while nocking an arrow. "I see riders."

"I see them, but wait until they are close enough for us to see if they are friends or foes."

Soon enough, the riders were in front of the gate. Looking for any sign of danger, Caldarian saw that they were goblins mounted on mountain goats and elves mounted on deer.

"This is captain Alathanir speaking," said Caldarian's father. "Who goes there?"

One brown-haired goblin rider broke from the group. Surveying him, Caldarian saw that he had a diamond brooch pinned to his breast which could only mean that he was an envoy of the goblin king.

"I am the new goblin ambassador to the humans," he said. "My name is Godirik."

"Open the gate," said Alathanir.

As the riders were entering the Outpost, Caldarian heard snatches of conversations.

"I hope you will find this place to your taste Lord Godirik," said an elf. "Our accommodations do not have the elven splendor or goblin sturdiness of our usual constructions."

"That will not be a problem," replied Godirik. "I have come to this planet for new discoveries and I think I will not be disappointed."

One hour later, the goblin guards in their blood-red armors arrived to replace the elves. As Caldarian walked toward his home, he smiled at the memories of how he had hated these human-like wooden houses that looked like nothing the elves or goblins built when he had been a child. Now that he was an adult and had spent most of his life there, he loved the Outpost and the way it served as a threshold between the worlds and as a bridge leading to prosperity for all.

Year 423 of the Age of Worlds-Crossing (1010 by human calendar)

Patrolling the wall, Caldarian stayed alert. While he had always taken his duties seriously, the last year had been full of events which, without directly affecting the lives of the Outpost's inhabitants, had cast a shadow over the area.

Despite himself, Caldarian shuddered as he recalled the reports he had heard of the human villages and towns in the surrounding lands being destroyed, with no traces remaining of their inhabitants.

Noticing a movement on the plain before the wall, Caldarian

snapped back into focus and signalled to his kinsmen. Nocking their bows, the elves aimed at the lone figure running toward the Outpost, ready to release their arrows if they judged it necessary.

Eventually, the runner resolved itself into a blond human, perhaps no older than sixteen years.

"Halt!" shouted Alathanir when the human was near enough. "State your business!"

"I need to speak with Lord Godirik!" shouted the human while frantically waving his arms. "I have a warning for him!"

"What kind of warning? What is your name?"

"My name is Tavey," replied the human. "You will soon be under attack."

"Do you think we can trust him?" asked Caldarian. "What if it is a trap?"

"If he is trying to deceive us, then he is a good actor," replied Alathanir. "Wait before the gate, human. We will join you shortly."

A few minutes later, the elves opened the gate, Caldarian aiming an arrow at the youngster. In reply, the human threw a sword onto the ground before the elves.

"I mean you no harm," he said. "I must speak with Godirik."

"Search him," said Alathanir to his warriors.

After having inspected the human for any concealed blade and finding none, Caldarian nodded to his father.

"Very well," replied Alathanir before gesturing for five warriors, including his son, to escort the human to the Hall.

As they walked, forming a circle around the human, Caldarian saw that his clothes were torn and his armor battered and covered with blood stains. When they reached the Hall, an elf knocked on the door of the goblin building. Immediately, a goblin opened the door and after a few words with the elves beckoned the human inside.

"Have you seen the look on his face?" asked one elf as they were returning to the wall.

"Yes," replied Caldarian. "Such fear. You would think he has seen a nightmare become real."

Standing on the wall in a line with his kinsmen, Caldarian waited.

"How is such a thing possible?" asked the warrior next to him. "What magic can animate the dead?"

"We are about to find out," replied Caldarian, trying to sound confidant despite the apprehension twisting his gut.

Eventually, an army became visible through the valley's entrance, like a snake appearing between two rocks. With each hour it crept closer until the elves could distinguish individuals among the attackers. Prayers to the World-Spirit resounded over the wall at the sight of the humans with glassy eyes and skin displaying the color of rotting flesh. All this confirmed that Tavey's words had not been an exaggeration and that his former lord's army truly consisted of hundreds of animated corpses.

Carrying a mixture of weapons or tools, the dead humans advanced toward the gate like cold air creeping on a house.

A clarion resounded and the elves raised their bows while the goblins did the same with their crossbows. As soon as their enemies were in range, the Outpost's two hundred defenders released their projectiles. To their horrors, the walking corpses were unaffected by the arrows and bolts that struck them like a hurricane, and kept advancing. The fireballs cast by the Outpost's elf mage did more damage, but still could not stop the attackers on their own.

A second volley followed with no more results; then a third, and a fourth. Some corpses stumbled and did not rise again for unknown reasons, but the bulk of their horde reached the wall unscathed and raised ladders, the tip of one hitting the crenellation right before Caldarian.

When a corpse reached the top, the elf struck with his sword, plunging it into the abomination's chest, praying that it would be enough. But like he had feared, the dead human was unaffected and swung a dagger at him, Caldarian raising his shark-fin shaped shield to block the attack. All around him, corpses were slowly but surely gaining ground on the wall despite being stabbed several times or even being dismembered with no visible effect.

Here and there, the screams of an elf or goblin resounded as the dead's weapons bit into living flesh. Being pushed back by the dead humans that followed his first opponent, Caldarian fought the urge to flee and kept hacking at his foes. A slash from his sword eventually severed the foremost creature's leg and it fell from the wall but the elf had no time to enjoy this victory as more corpses attacked him.

Blocking a swipe from an axe, Caldarian saw too late a hammer aiming for his head. Jumping on his left, he avoided a blow to his skull but the attack still struck him on the shoulder. His armor endured but the pain disorientated him. Before he could recover, the corpse pinned him against the crenellations with one hand while raising his hammer for another strike. In desperation, Caldarian thrust with a scream, the tip of his sword punching though the dead human's mouth and erupting from the back of his skull.

Immediately, the corpse stumbled to the ground.

Shock and relief clashing in his mind, Caldarian remembered his other dead foe with the axe. Snapping back into focus, the elf swung his sword. The steel sliced through rotten flesh and bone, severing the human's head from his corpse which stumbled at once.

"Aim for their heads," he shouted as he pierced another dead human's brain.

His words were repeated over the entire wall and the tide of the battle turned at once. In a matter of minutes, the attackers were driven back, their heads cut from their bodies or pierced by steel.

Just as Caldarian's heart filled with hope that they may survive this night, a lightning bolt erupted from the undead horde and struck the gate, destroying it in a shower of wood, stone and defenders sent flying over the houses.

"Retreat to the Hall!" shouted Godirik.

With discipline, the surviving goblins and elves left the wall and formed a shield line before the Hall where the civilians had taken shelter. The undead kept coming but were now cut down like wheat by the defenders' steel. Even the living humans that joined the fray were swiftly defeated.

Just as victory seemed a certainty, an armored human moved to the fore of the army and extended his arms, projecting lightning bolts that killed elves and goblins by the dozen. To his credit, the elf mage conjured protective shining spheres around his allies but they were smashed aside by the human's raw power. From the corner of his eyes, Caldarian saw a bolt strike his father, reducing him to a charred corpse instantly.

Even as he screamed in anguish, a crossbow shot resounded and the human wizard stumbled, a bolt burrowed to the fletching in his shoulder. Taking advantage of his distraction, the elf mage projected a shockwave that struck the wizard like a meteor, sending his helm flying and revealing silver hair.

At this sight, a gasp of horror swept over the defenders as they remembered the stories and realised what they were facing.

Wizard-Lord! thought Caldarian with a gulp of fear as he realized that they would need a miracle to defeat such a foe.

Before anyone could react, the human Tavey charged forward, sword in the hand. Before his swipe could connect with the Wizard-Lord's neck, another human identical to him tackled him. Rolling before jumping back on his feet, Tavey met his attacker with a look of pure hatred in his eyes.

"Charge!" shouted Godirik as dead and living humans came forward to surround the wounded Wizard-Lord.

Preceded by fireballs flying from the elf mage's staff, the remaining elves and goblins surged forward, piercing or slicing the skulls of all opponents in their path until their sorcerous foe was almost within reach. But even as they destroyed his last slaves, the Wizard-Lord ripped the bolt from his body, his flesh healing, before extending his hands.

At once, Caldarian's body stopped moving despite himself and he could only watch as the Wizard-Lord advanced toward Godirik, muttering words that the elf could not hear. Just as the human raised his blade to strike down the goblin, Godirik's flesh suddenly blazed with light and lightning bolts erupted from his hands, forcing the Wizard-Lord to conjure a magical sphere around himself.

Caldarian's body stumbled as he recovered control of himself but like every other warrior, he could not move, transfixed by the magical fight in front of him. For more than a minute, it seemed that Godirik's attack could not overcome the defense of the human but eventually the latter jumped on his side, barely avoiding the bolts. Extending a hand, the human Wizard-Lord made his follower that looked so much like Tavey fly toward him. Once he had grabbed him, he disappeared again. Immediately, Godirik collapsed.

As the sun rose over the ravaged village, all quietly gasped as they saw that Godirik's hair had gone from brown to silver.

Year 433 of the Age of Worlds-Crossing (1020 by human calendar)

"I can't believe we are doing this," said Caldarian as he looked down on the valley from the slope leading to the Rift leading back to the Homeworld. "Even if the goblin king ordered it, it is wrong."

"It is for the best, my son," replied his mother. "With this human Wizard-Lord, Alastair, declaring war on the goblins, Islelders and Homeworld-born humans, we should suspend relations with the humans for now."

"Father died defending the Outpost. Abandoning it amounts to making his death pointless."

"He died in battle, protecting those who could not fight. He died like every warrior should. Also, thanks to you, we now know how to fight the Animated."

Tears coursed on Caldarian's tears as the elvish building collapsed. The figure standing in front of it turned toward the goblin building and cast a series of shockwaves and lightning bolts that quickly reduced it to rumble.

For more than an hour, Caldarian, his mother, and every elf and goblin who had survived the battle ten years before, watched as the Wizard-Lord Godirik used his new powers to destroy the colony they had painfully built long ago.

The Outpost was supposed to symbolize a golden age for humans, Islelders and goblins, he thought with a gulp. *Now its ruins are just a reminder of how everything we dreamt of regarding Earth has led to nothing except for the coming war against the Wizard-Lord Alastair.*

Once the wall itself had been reduced to dust, a flash illuminated the slope where they stood. When it disappeared, Godirik stood, its silver eyes blazing with fury.

"It is done," he said. "Our time on Earth is over. The Age of Worlds-Crossing is ended."

Without waiting for a reply, the goblin headed for the cave containing the rift, followed by his kinsmen and the elves.

Caldarian cast a last mournful look at the ruins of his former home, reflecting on everything that had been lost, before leaving behind the light of the Earth's sun and heading to a place he no longer considered home.

Author's Note

This short story takes place in the canon of a yet unpublished series entitled "The Wizards'Game".

THE COLONIST

Randal Heide

The common area was dark and deserted when Vahva exited the lift from the habitation stacks above. He had never seen it like this; all the shops and bars shuttered. He was always in bed this early on a Sunday. Apparently, so was everyone else – which was what he'd counted on.

Reaching a nondescript door to the outside, he checked his air kit and took a whiff from his nostril line before stepping through, just as the warning sign recommended. There was nothing poisonous to humans in the planet's air; there just wasn't nearly enough oxygen in it yet. At the current rate of increase, it wouldn't be breathable for decades.

The sun was just creeping up over the horizon, casting a harsh light that struck him as far more unEarthly than the light of midday. He'd noticed before that, for some reason, this sun's slightly bluish tone was much more pronounced at sunset. Apparently at sunrise too; this was the first he'd witnessed.

He picked his way through the rocky scree down to the rough path along the water's edge. There was a proper road to where he was going, but this way was much more direct. Way off on the far bank of the wide river, the sun shone cold and blue on barren, lifeless rock. Even with all the billions still to come from Earth, he figured they'd probably never build over there. There were too many habitable worlds out here, many of them with more than enough room for everyone.

To his left, the habitation towered above him as he followed the riverbank; a neat, orderly, massive pile of prefab boxes, assembled into one big box and plunked onto the rock like a package that had just been set down for a moment. For some reason it had been painted a sickly yellow ochre that managed to clash horribly with the golden tan of the rock. He wondered why they'd bothered to paint it at all; was it perhaps to ward off some sort of radiation exposure they hadn't bothered to warn people about?

As he rounded a bend, the water taxi dock came into view up ahead. Instinctively, he patted his pocket. The box was there, of course, right where he'd put it. And the taxi dock looked deserted - perfect.

At the dock entrance, he presented the PersPak strapped to his arm to the terminal, and a gate opened. Stepping onto the nearest taxi, he said "Public Works dock", and the boat eased away into the river. He had to laugh at himself, recalling how long it had taken him to realize how easy this was. The taxis wouldn't take him where he ultimately wanted to go; that wasn't an established stop. The Works had what he needed to get there, but the problem of getting in – with its secure entrance and three-metre tall perimeter fence - had stumped him for weeks, until he'd noticed a taxi dropping some workers off at the jetty out in back. So, he'd tried it once himself, just a dry run, intending to pretend that the taxi had misunderstood his command if anyone accosted him. But no one had even noticed as the taxi pulled up. He could have just walked right off onto the docks, but he had no reason to that day, and didn't want to draw attention to himself.

On this morning, he did step off. It had only been a short ride, barely four hundred metres down the river, but already the warmth of the water and sunlight was beating down the nighttime

chill. He felt a moment of panic as his eye caught movement
somewhere in the clutter of the yard behind the main building, but
whoever it was wasn't paying any attention to the dock area and
didn't reappear. Still, Varhva moved quickly. He didn't need much
time here; and once he was gone, he didn't care if someone came
after him, as long as he had a decent head start.

A variety of watercraft was moored at the jetty, but Varhva
didn't hesitate. He already knew what he wanted – one of the little
skiffs used for any variety of light, one or two-person jobs. There
were several of them here, and, as he'd hoped, there was no security
at all. They were just tied up to the dock, no locks or ID scanners,
with motors and lifejackets in place, ready for use. He selected one
that looked a little cleaner than the others and set out. Yes,
technically he was committing theft, but it felt right somehow.
After all, how many times had he applied to come out here to do
ecosystem work? They shouldn't have kept turning him down; he
should have been here as an employee. Maybe then, things would
have turned out differently.

Of course he knew why they hadn't, but that just showed how
stupid the whole thing was; how they were getting everything
wrong. So he'd had some depression issues. Surely, as Earth's
ecosystem slid steadily towards collapse all around them, that only
placed him in the majority. And especially for someone like him, an
animal husbandry specialist – well, who wouldn't have felt a bit
down, watching the majority of Earth's species become functionally
extinct within a single lifetime? And besides, unlike so many back
home, he'd really *wanted* to come; even after Leuchtterm had
breached the infowall; revealing what conditions in the colonies
were really like, and that it was an irrevocable one-way trip. When
they'd finally got the first megatransports into service and initiated

the lottery system to increase the flow rate, justice had been served. He'd been one of the first winners.

A warm, salty breeze was picking up off the ocean, and the water, which had been smooth as glass, was beginning to get a little choppy. He adjusted his course slightly, to head straight into the wind until he was further into the lee of the delta islands. He was perfectly comfortable in a boat like this; he'd used similar ones many times back home on Earth. Up ahead rose the profile of the Model City, backlit by the morning sun. Now, *this* was the New Venice he'd been promised. Of course, since he'd come on a lottery pass, he hadn't picked it. Still, he might have, if he'd been given a choice.

This was the city that appeared in all the PR photos back home. Sure, it was all still just simple prefab boxes hiding under a thin veneer of faux Venetian Gothic styling. But they had at least mixed it up a bit, changing colours and sizes, and had kept it all to no more than a few floors tall. And there really were 'canals'; the natural channels separating the three islands it was built on. For a colony, it truly was rather nice, even though there wasn't so much as a blade of grass to be seen.

The problem was, it only had capacity for the few thousand corp and government types who both lived and worked there. The reality for everyone else – the nearly 300,000 idle, pointless, air-and-food consuming souls on Basic – was the habitation that he'd left behind upriver. They were allowed to visit the Model City, of course – if they could scrape together enough for a meal in one of the restaurants or whatever. But for them, there was no hope of ever living or working there. The colony only needed a few thousand employees to function. Everyone else was either a hair artist or totally useless. Well, maybe not *totally* useless – as long as you fed them, they did at least keep producing soil. Soil that, one day, would drive a terraforming process that would translate this lifeless rock ball into a new, improved version of Earth.

Yeah, right. Vahva didn't have a Ph D (another reason they hadn't picked him earlier), but he had enough basic science training to recognize – once he'd arrived here, at least – just how far-fetched that dream was. You could dump a hundred year's worth of their collected composted shit onto the rocks around the hab stacks, and after the first good rain, it would all be washed out to sea. So, okay, that might still help a bit – the microbes they'd seeded into the ocean to produce oxygen would probably like it – but seriously... This planet had roughly three times the volume of surface water as Earth.

There were other boats out on the water now, but just a handful. None seemed the least bit interested in him, but he gave them a wide berth anyways. Following the shoreline as he rounded the city, he found himself watching the "tide rim", which was visible now that the tide was going out. All along the waterline, everywhere, was a perfect, unbroken rim of mineral deposits formed by countless millions of years of steady, uninterrupted tidal action. It was about forty cems from top to bottom here; the exact variation between local high and low tides, and it projected at least a dozen cems out from the bare rock it was bonded to. Originally, it had been a pale yellow colour, but now it was stained with a dark, greasy slime. Vahva knew that was probably a permanent change now. He wondered whether it was still a relatively local phenomenon, or whether the oxygen-producing bacterial life in the water had spread around the planet already.

The thought made him aware of the box in his pocket again. This time, he pulled it out and opened it, to check on them. The roaches inside were fine – of course. An hour inside a warm, dark box was heavenly to them. He'd been disappointed to find that absolutely no pets, of any kind, were allowed on board the transports. They even screened all passengers for lice. For a scientific expedition to a pristine new world, that made sense – but wasn't the whole point now to colonize? To regrow a new Earth out of the decaying, near-dead tissue of the old?

He hadn't been without animals of some kind to care for since... well, he couldn't remember a time, all the way back to his earliest childhood. That had probably been the worst part of the voyage for him – worse even than the crowding, the horrible food, the smells, and the unbelievable boredom. He hadn't know it at the time, but that had merely been preparation for a lifetime spent in the hab stacks, where the only difference was that he had his little twelve square metre cell all to himself, with his own personal sink and toilet.

So, when he'd discovered the roaches on board (surprise, surprise – of course *they'd* find a way through the screening), he did what came naturally, and collected about a dozen of them. Throughout the rest of the voyage, and all the long, dark months since, they'd been his companions - his only link to self and sanity.

Now, as he rounded the west side of the Model City, his ultimate destination came into view. It was another island – a rough, jutting spire of rock set off a ways from the others; too steep and rough to bother building on. And now, heading out of the shelter of the City islands, he felt the full ocean breeze in his face, strong and fresh. For the first time since leaving Earth, Vahva felt alive; excited. He'd felt better ever since coming up with this idea – good enough to drag himself out of bed for once, shave and shower even, and to venture out and figure out how to implement it. But he hadn't felt like this since – again, he couldn't remember when.

Certainly, it had been years – decades, even. And he knew that if he'd stayed home to watch Earth die, he'd never have felt like this again. So, okay – it was a good thing that he'd come, after all.

No one followed him as he headed out across the channel to the big rock. No one was waiting there for him as he rounded it, revealing a side and a shoreline that he'd never seen. That was the only potential flaw in the plan – what if there was no good place to land? It was awfully rough and rocky. But although the water was choppy, the long, curving arm of the outer peninsula sheltered the entire lagoon, so at least there was no open ocean swell. Eventually he found a nook with a rock face that sloped gently up and away from the water, and put in there.

The sun was well clear of the horizon now, and it was warm and peaceful here. The rock was pleasantly cool to the touch, and the familiar sound of the water lapping against the shore was comforting. He knelt down and studied the area; all around were deep, dark fissures in the rock, some with water lapping into them lower down. Perfect.

He took the box out of his pocket and set it down on the rocks. Then he knelt at the water's edge, reached down, and wiped some of the dark brown slime off the waterline mineral rim. His finger came away dirty, leaving a bright, off-white streak of clean crust. Carefully, he opened the box, wiped the slime off his finger onto one of the inside surfaces, and watched for a bit. The roaches seemed interested in it. How could they not? Decaying organic matter was the stuff of life for them.

But he was pretty sure they wouldn't like the light right here. So he took the box over to a crack, a good deep one with water at the bottom and a healthy portion of slime-coated tidal crust, and tipped the box over to let the roaches go. He was surprised how fast they moved; they disappeared down into the dark recesses of the crack within seconds. Oh, well, that was okay, it just meant they liked the place.

Then, he returned to a sunny, comfortable spot on the rock. He removed the feed line from his nostril, then took off the air kit. He tore the line from the kit, and threw it out as far as he could into the water. He found a loose rock, and smashed the kit itself with it. Then, already feeling dizzy, he sat down to die.

He felt okay as he faded out. Out of dire necessity, Earth's lifeforms were colonizing the Universe. It was no place for him, but at least he'd been able to play his part.

Author's Note

If you asked me to sum up what inspires me to write, I would have to say it's the stuff I hate most about the stuff I love most. And as a child of the 60's, it probably goes without saying that I owe my love of sci-fi to Star Trek The Original Series. Shatner's Kirk might have been a father figure to me, if I hadn't had a perfectly good one of my own already. But still, far be it from me to suggest that The Original Series wasn't, ahem, a little uneven in quality at times. Even more so, the blockbuster movies that followed in the 70's.

So if, like me, you found the capability of the Genesis terraforming device from Star Trek III: The Search for Spock to be ridiculously implausible, you will probably get this story. Thanks for checking it out.

THE LIVING TREE

Twinkles

We lived on the Western side of the hill.

I knew we couldn't speak of the Eastern side, but Marsha was already angry. I might as well implore on it. I had secretly ventured to the Eastern end of the shores last night. It had a loud swoosh that travelled up to the middle of the hill. Its massive waves of thunder left an impression on me. The Western end that was so very familiar to us all, was entirely opposite in its calm and almost serene scenery.

It was true, everything I heard about it. On the Eastern side, the hill leaned in close to the shoreline, and the massive waves threw everything into the rocky slopes and killed all that tried. It had also an uplifting energy that made me feel alive.

Marsha demanded, "You know exactly how it works. You had to be right there at the right time!"

I was getting yelled at by Marsha. I didn't like it.

"Have you ever been to the Eastern shore?" I asked. I wasn't expecting an answer, because I saw her wave to the guard and the big key was brought out to unlock the big door that would keep me from getting down the hill that night. I was going to be locked in until the next day. I had never been locked away before, never missed a night of going down to the islands below. In fact, the rusty keyhole felt suspicious as it squeaked and turned to let me in.

"The massive waves…" I tried, hoping the guard would bear to listen. Of course not, I was a prisoner for the day. I wouldn't be joining the rest of the hill colony that night. They would jump at seven evening. Sharp. As the sun was setting. That was the time those hill-creatures always rose to the surface of the western shore, like floats to catch our fall. Everybody jumped at seven. Every creature floated at seven. When we landed on them, they would swim us towards the island where there was abundant food and adventure. I would be the only one left up on the hill that night.

My back rested on the rough and cold floor. It was dead silent. I had never been alone up on the hill before. It was covered in rocks and sand. Nothing could grow here except the living tree and us. We had to get downhill every night to gather food. We couldn't store any livestock or food supplies – the creatures would know of our plunder and the colony would be destroyed.

In order for us to all make the jump, we had to find fresh skin that would glide our jump down the hill into a smooth sail. This skin was found only from the sap of the living tree. Well, the colony called it the living tree. It grew only on the hill, and everyone who wanted to get down to gather food would need to have their own living tree to ensure their own survival.

And if we lost our own tree, we lost our lives.

My brother Mike was the first person in the hill who had ever spoken about the Eastern shore. They said it was the reason why we were stuck. And whenever someone spoke about it, the creatures would stop coming to fetch us from below. Everyone was frightened from speaking about it. I was scared of Mike too. Mike had lost his living tree that night he went missing. He was the one gone rogue.

Every day, the tribe brought them to the sacred hole. Marsha had a perfect plan. The fresh skin that we used to get downhill would dry up and the next day we had to bring it to the sacred hole.

Twinkles

I was assigned the task of collecting the skin to the secret path of
escape. I was the chosen one, I was told. Nobody else should know,
for they thought that when they brought the skin to the sacred hole,
the creatures collected them every night. The folks all knew that the
skin was the way of life around the hill. It became in itself a sacred
kind of property. It kept us safe.

By night, I collected them, dried, and ready to build onto the
escape path. I was entrusted with an extraordinary feat - the secret
hole led to the island and I had to lay the skins around the hole so
that it would eventually cover the route to become big enough as
our path of safe escape. We would no longer be trapped in the hill.
We had the sap from the tree that would glide us safely down the
hill. Why wouldn't I be proud of the great thing I'm doing for my
tribesmen and women?

Now I lie on the cold hard ground, worried about what I'd
done, missing my daily task last night. It was hot and musky inside
this tall and empty cell. I heard the sound of the waves again and I
shivered. "You've got to make the choice." It said. "You've got to
make the choice!" It got louder. And louder. Then I shivered even
more, because it was apparent that I was going to die. I don't know
what I had done to myself, all because I had missed the time Marsha
needed me to deliver the skins. I did choose to follow my entrusted
duties. I was special, so I was told, to do this alone.

I'm going to die now, like Mike. I had spoken about the
Eastern Shores, and ventured there. This taboo would make me lose
my living tree, as Mike lost his that night he disappeared having
spoken about the Eastern shores. I had missed Marsha's perfect
plan, I probably deserved it. I saw the whole chain of slaughter
happening because of me. I was excited when my neighbour was
expecting. The assignment of the living tree to her baby was also

dependant on Marsha. I was always blackmailed, using the life and death of babies and the development of the escape path as a measuring tool, since living trees took time to mature their sap.

Marsha would unlikely let me be her runner again. I knew something nobody else did. Her lie to the rest of the colony was not safe with me, and she knew that. She wouldn't let me reveal what really happened to the dried skins, that the creatures never took it. If I didn't get myself out, I had better lock myself in really good.

I reached the rusty catch of the door handle and my skins-blade. I didn't think the blade would cut through the metal no matter how rusty it was, but when it came off I guess it chose for me. I ran back to the secret path, where it was laid with dried skins till it met midway downhill. It had stayed at that level for a long time. The creatures, they took them in the morning, I was told. We had to lay them faster than they were taken. We couldn't afford to miss a single day.

I climbed down, holding my blade in my hand. I didn't know what else to do, because I heard a sound. Someone was removing the skins. Our eyes met, I held my blade up to attack him.

•

"It's me, it's Mike!" I heard him speak.

"If you're Mike why are you stealing our skins? Mike is dead!" I said, realising that he sounded exactly like Mike. I stepped in closer, watching carefully as my blade closed in on his neck. The man never retaliated.

I was allowed to scrutinise his face and then the truth hit me. It was my brother!

"I knew you wouldn't hurt me. I know you." Mike said. "You know the problem with these skins, from the sap of the living tree?"

"They are from the living trees, the life currency of our tribe. What's the problem?" I said.

"The sap." Mike replied.

"Yea it's a special sap?"

"The thing kills the natural enzymes in the water. The creatures – do you know why they always break your fall?"

"Because they want to help us to the island, and we supply them the skins."

"Wrong."

"What do you mean, wrong?"

"Because the sap from the skins would kill the water and the island would die along with it."

"The creatures would kill us, Mike, why would they save us?"

"They're not trying to kill you or save you, brother, they're trying to save themselves."

I paused.

"Don't you see? There is no life on the hill? All other green life ceases to exist, besides the living tree."

"I never thought about it." I concurred.

"What do you think will happen when the sap skins reach the bottom of the hill?" Mike asked.

"Look, I don't know what you're talking about." I said.

"If you don't know what enzymes are, it's okay. You don't need to know. But the chemical balance of losing the natural enzymes in a body of water can cause tremendous life loss. Sea creatures would die, fishes would no longer swim here, and then the creatures would die along with them. From what I know, it would become a disaster." Mike said.

He then brought me to the Eastern part of the hill, where nobody from the hill had ever been.

"Do you know how to get down without the skins? Do you want to live in the island forever?" Mike asked. He looked over the edge of the hill down into the waves.

I was scared, it was too late to go back. I was definitely going to lose my living tree and be killed by Marsha. But I didn't want to jump like Mike looked like he was about to. My horns started glowing like Mike's, and I looked at my feet. All three toes wouldn't budge, wanting to stand still.

"You've got to make the choice." Mike said, exactly as I had heard midway downhill. With one hop, he leapt and fell down from the edge.

"And jump!"

"Mike!!!" I yelled after him as I carried my heavy feet to the edge of the hill.

I saw Mike flying free, with open wings.

"Mike? What happened?" I yelled.

"Make the choice, jump, and follow me brother! Find your wings. That's who we are. Don't let Marsha shut you off from your wings." Mike hovered up and down from the hill to the shore, and then I saw the others.

There were many of us down there, waiting on the Eastern shore, waiting for me as I hesitated, trying to cling on to any comfort I could grasp up on the hill as they continued cajoling me.

"What would you choose?"

I wasn't prepared to face the possibility of a fight with my own people one day, or with Marsha. I didn't like what I saw when I imagined what the future would be, my tribe being divided. I guess it already was. It didn't split because of the choices made by the folks like Mike. It wasn't wrong to choose. What was wrong, was what truly was happening up here on the hill, and the lies. There

Twinkles

was truth to be revealed.

And the first truth I saw as the dust showered the hill, were my own wings.

Author's Note

There was a lot left to be explored, yet to be left ambiguous so that a reader would make their own conclusions. For e.g., why would Marsha do something like that? I didn't want to make the characters sound really more inhuman so I didn't change the names as suggested to tribal or alien ones. Guess what, species are not all that different in terms of personality and survival. I didn't want to predict and restrict Marsha's motives. But I knew what I wanted. Hopefully you would make a choice too by the ending of the story.

There was absolutely a lot that could be improved in the sequence and editing of the story as well. I had chosen to let it rest. Thank you for reading.

THE TEST

Catherine Oyiliagu

Author's Caution: Strong language

The pyramid on Lake Ontario was a behemoth. The size of a small mountain, it housed the entire city of 10 million inhabitants. Commerce, agriculture, mineral extraction...everything worth doing was done there. In one location. No more long commutes. And the frigid weather six months out of the year? There was no need to worry about that either.

Somewhere in its center, a procession wound its way along several long hallways. There didn't appear to be a leader of any sort, yet the procession was orderly and the people walked purposefully, each person eventually stopping before a nondescript door.

Rebecca stood before her door and eyed it carefully, the way one would eye a sleeping predator. Yet she felt no fear; only excitement, even though this would be the most important test of her life; of all their lives.

It could be because she'd never experienced an examination before, and wasn't aware of the proper emotions to feel. According to human history, in the time Before Ra, testing began at a young age, much younger than her - than their - twenty-five years. It involved the regurgitation of memorized words, phrases and numbers using pen and paper, and in later years keystrokes, virtually every few months after a child turned five until their twenties. It was, Rebecca was told, a torturous exercise approached with fear, trepidation, and tears. Schooling then, was a terrible, horrible, no good, very bad thing most people had to endure. That was the human way. Fortunately, the Ririans arrived, and eventually did away with such backwards thinking. And the Ririan way was so much better. "School" - if you could call it that - was akin to a computer game - an interactive simulation where you learned and progressed by solving increasingly difficult problems. Any testing was organic and nothing to be afraid of. Why couldn't humans have come up with something like that?

The door slid open soundlessly, and Rebecca stepped forward. She felt like she'd been waiting for this moment her whole life, and her heart was about to burst open with anticipation. This was the ultimate test - the only test - that could separate her from the rest of her kind and show the Ririans that she was more than a drone. If she passed, she could become an Administrator. Maybe even a Tower Supervisor, a job no human had ever held. Other people may be content with their lot, lazing about during the day, drinking, partying, fucking, drugging, living the "high life;" and operating Bot Generators at night, literally as they slept. That was the only "job" required of humans - 8 hours each of neural power to run the massive factories that manufactured the robots that did all the work. But Rebecca wanted more out of life. She needed to have a purpose. She needed to move up from the cramped quarters of the lower decks to the panoramic views of the upper decks, and this once-in-a-lifetime exam by the Ririans was the only opportunity to prove her mettle.

She glanced around, and found herself on the bridge of a spaceship. Simulated, of course.

"Captain on the bridge," one of the silhouetted figures said, and the crew rose.

"As you were," Rebecca said, making sure her voice was

nuanced and authoritative. She walked to the Captain's chair and took a seat.

Silence.

Were they waiting for her orders? What orders?

"Report!" she barked.

"We've made a long-range sweep of the Obsidian Sector, and have located an inhabited planet."

"On screen."

She recognized the blue planet as soon as it came up on the viewscreen. Earth. Was this a First Contact simulation on the discovery of Earth? The arrival that preceded the Ririan's colonization of the planet?

But it wouldn't do to assume. Administrators don't assume. They analyze the data and make their conclusions.

"What did the scans reveal?"

She listened as another Silhouette read out the planet's parameters: size, atmosphere, stability, population (9 billion), technological and social advancements (Level 2: carbon-burning, nuclear-carrying, non-egalitarian; barely civilized by Ririan standards)...

"How shall we proceed, Captain?"

So was that the test? If so, it was indeed the First Contact simulation. How to proceed... Well, how does one proceed with children?

"We must tread carefully," she said, "understand the regional conflicts and offer solutions; appear as unthreatening as possible. Be respectful. Scan the airwaves. Let us study this planet we have come upon."

The simulation sped up. First contact came via Earth's foremost space agency - NASA - with a response signal to their listening devices, and the expected cliches of "we come in peace" and "take us to your leader." There was much jubilation and ego-trotting by the inhabitants of that part of the planet, most of whom had nothing to do with it. But jubilation was soon followed by a great deal of diplomatic wrangling, countries jostling amongst each other to be the first to welcome aliens from outer space. To end the dispute, Rebecca graciously suggested a meeting at the United Nations. "We would be honored to land our ships on the grounds of a convention, where every nation is represented. That is our foremost request."

The room dimmed, and one after another, the Silhouettes disappeared.

Was that it? Did she pass? She wondered.

Her chair moved backwards and a round table appeared before her. Other Silhouettes materialized, seated around it.

"We've completed negotiations with a number of countries and have begun building the towers," the figure at the far end said. "The humans are calling them pyramids; some are even claiming that we're ancient aliens returning to a planet we once called home."

"If we can use that to our advantage, we should," Rebecca interrupted. "I believe having some historical claim to land is of value in this society."

The figure nodded, before continuing. "The negotiations so far have been with Niger and Chad - the tower … pyramid …. in the Sahara is taking shape. We also have a lease on the North Pole, and another in the heavily forested regions of the Amazon. Excellent, strategic locations for us, yes. However, we need to be closer to more heavily populated centers of the planet."

The silence lengthened and stretched. Rebecca guessed that was her cue.

"Are there schematics on our preferred locations?" she asked.
"Yes."

A three dimensional hologram of Earth descended from the ceiling, displaying the various sites - at least one on each continent, either on or close to bodies of water, and human populations in the millions.

"There's bound to be resistance to our building so close to population centers," the figure said.

"Not to mention that a few cities will flood when we build on their lakes, seas and oceans. Unlike humans, we cannot abide any casualties."

Rebecca thought for a moment longer. She needed to offer a solution, not just to the Ririans, but something that would meet the needs of the humans as well - at least on the surface. "In gratitude," she began, "for the...generous allotment of land for Ririan habitats...let us offer to build free homes for their homeless peoples, illegals and refugees close to, but not quite at their population centers. It would certainly take those...problems off their hands and allow us greater involvement in their government's activities. We will of course allow their engineers and...media to visit - to prove that our manner of building is environmentally sound and non-polluting."

Okay, so far so good. But how to leverage... "Given the natural greed of humans, even those who could afford their own homes will cry out for our handouts, and as the need grows, we will add units to the pyramids. Slowly. Those dissenters will be our means of weathering whatever pushback might come our way."

The Silhouettes faded, and the scene changed once more.
Was that it? Did she pass?
In reality, she had no idea how the Ririans had come to rule

Earth. It wasn't something that was covered at school in any detail. She vaguely recalled that the Ririans had been a civilizing influence, turning a war-torn planet into a peaceful one where every single human had access to as much food and booze and sex and drugs as they wanted. Except the rebels - savages that lived outside the pyramids and rejected the Ririan way. Rebecca had spotted one once from a window, paddling away along the flooded streets of the ruins of Toronto, scavenging scrap from the giant gravestones that humans used to live in.

Where was she now, and what was she looking at? Standing, she leaned against the railing of the balustrade. Loud voices rang out from the promenade. A human male was yelling at a bot, trying to prevent its entry into his unit.

"Something about his right to bear arms," the Silhouette beside her said. "The bot has been instructed to take away his guns and a few other weapons found during the last scan."

Exhaustion must have crept in by then because Rebecca lost her temper. Here was a man who had been given a free home, free food and the opportunity to live a carefree existence, but who still wanted the means to end the life of another. Savages!

She stepped into one of the descending platforms to the lower floor and approached the irate human.

"I understand you do not wish for this bot to confiscate your guns."

He glared at her, red faced and sweaty, skin so unlike the smooth, silver-like hues of the Ririans.

"You may keep your guns," she said. "Outside the pyramid." And she turned and walked away. Yes, go back to the existence of your dead-end job; your constant worry over debt and money; the ever present danger of an accident or crime that could take your life...go back to that if your guns mean so much to you.

The images around her faded - the Silhouette, promenade and people - but a new scene didn't appear. Just the large, white, circular room she had first walked into. Had she blown it? Had she failed? The Ririans were a controlled and civilized people. Anger had no place in their society. They were never curt; never used brute force. They were like placid water that slowly eroded even the most formidable rock.

Taking a deep breath, she spoke out loud. "I apologize for my temper. It won't happen again."

The screen shimmered, another scene beginning to take shape. It seemed the test would continue. Good. Because she wasn't done yet. Not by a long shot. She would pass. She would prove herself. But she couldn't have known or understood the consequences, because if Rebecca had looked down at herself at that moment, she may have been startled at the lustre emanating from her skin, and its increasing silver hue.

Author's Note

In this story, I attempted to explore one possible outcome of an extraterrestrial colonization of our planet. What if an advanced alien species decided to make Earth a colony? Unlike most takes of an alien invasion, my approach was that of a gradual take over without violence; one that centered on a slow, careful and insidious indoctrination that had the power to turn humans against their own way of thinking and being. Whether this made things better or worse is up to the reader to decide.

THE BITER BIT

Clesis Leran

A lush jungle greeted George as he set foot on the ground and walked deeper into the wild. The air was humid, more humid than his homeland. Big trees with unfamiliar shapes clouded the sun. Despite the protection offered by this canopy and his black cocked hat, he was already sweating profusely. Studded leather may not have been the brightest idea. But better safe than sorry thought James. After all, his people did not discover the new world; it had been claimed by the Vos Empire a few decades ago. And his job was to make sure that no Vos would interfere with the landing. *Find their forts and make sure you're unseen had said Constable Geralt.*

As stealthily as he could, he moved deeper and deeper into the jungle, leaving marks that he hoped would not be found by the Vos sentries. He had not seen any until then but you never knew. His kind had fled death and he would make sure that death befell any living creature that would stand in their way.

A few hours of wandering had left him with wonder and awe. The jungle was filled with life and its colors. The trees looked bigger and greener, the soil was covered with all kind of plants and fungi, the air rhymed with the sounds of a multitude of birds and animals. He had not experienced something similar since the Teutons had unleashed the Blight upon to Mercia. And even then, the forests of the rainy land were no match to this wealth of growth and abundance. George felt a touch of euphoria and excitement ran through his body. He thought about the endless possibilities that would open for his kind. They could make this haven into their new home, grow fields of vegetables, feed their sheep and cows, prosper and multiply, and most of all prepare for the time where the Tyrant of Mercia will catch up with them. As he cut into a strange shaped yellow fruit and inhaled the sweet fragrance that came out of it, he could almost smell victory.However, his daydreaming was short lived.

It had been too quick and too faint for it to be natural, a small snap quickly muffled not far from him. Hellbent on not raising suspicion from whoever was stalking him, George moved forward and continued to inspect his surroundings. Now that he knew that he was not alone, he only had to find a way to prompt his would-be hunter to make a mistake. He slowly increased his pace, looking for a tree big enough to hide his next movements. George did not have to wait too long to find a massive oak that would do the job. As he passed by it, he jumped sideways and climbed as fast as he could. The moss covering the tree made it slippery to ascend and he had to put more force into it. He stopped around 15 feet above the ground and waited for his opponent to follow his footsteps. He almost missed the slight ruffle that went through the grass as his hunter reached the base of the oak. Impressed by the skill of his opponent, George did not waste any time studying him. He gave a strong push with his legs against the bark and used the added momentum of the fall to slam down onto his foe. He felt a few cracks as his body crushed his target mercilessly to the ground, followed by a loud cry of pain and a rush of movements as George felt his prey trying to slip away from him. For goodness sake, he punched a few times in the not yet still body, intent on weakening it more than killing it.

"Stop struggling if you want to live." said George in the best growled Vos that he could muster. The Vos went still which confirmed George's accurate guess about this enemy nature.

"Now, you are going to turn very slowly. If you try anything funny, I will knife you down. Understood?" he asked.

A backward nod preceded the slow rolling of the Vos and George eased it by releasing some of the pressure. A haunted face came into his field of vision. It displayed the typical features of the Vos: copper skin, dark hair, black eyes, and round lines. George was surprised by the aged face of his prisoner, he looked to be in his late fifties but that did not match the stealth he has previously demonstrated. And there was something too familiar for him to not feel some kind of discomfort, he could read despair in every line of his enemy's face.

"Where is your camp? How many sentries? How many men? Tell the truth and I will claim you as my prisoner. Lie and you will not see another day." asked George.

His prisoner laughed hysterically. It was so out of place that George stayed speechless for a few seconds. He came to his sense and used a universal language to express his disapprovement; one punch for the disagreement and another one for good measure. The laughter stopped and the Vos spat a tooth.

In a deranged voice, he said: "It does not matter anymore! They're all dead inside. They're all his. And the same will happen to you if you don't run away. There is nothing but death in this godforsaken land."

"Stop this nonsense and answer my questions. I don't have time for your superstitious nonsense. Don't make me repeat myself." said George in a voice low with the promise of death.

"There used to be twenty sentries. They don't use them anymore. That's why I was able to flee... We...they are two hundred strong. The camp is still fifteen miles away, west." replied the Vos.

This back and forth went on as George asked more and more details about the Vos outpost. The Vos did not oppose any resistance and George was surprised by the smoothness of its interrogation. He could only see resignation in the face of his captive as he spilled more and more information on his kind. He felt his contempt building slowly towards the Vos. He had always despised deserters and their kind. As the interrogation neared its end, he knew it was time to end it before this coward started spurting lies again. In a quick motion, George drew his knife and pushed it to the hilt in the Vos body. He felt no resistance as flesh gave way and blood started to spill. The Vos looked stunned for a few seconds and as he breathed his last, George saw relief in his face.

George resumed his walk west and soon enough the wild jungle gave way to fields filled with a mixture of strange vegetables and familiar livestock. George felt again this sweet euphoria as he envisioned the potential of this place for his people. After a few more miles, he followed a man-made track that led him all the way to the Vos outpost. Organized in a square structure, it was surrounded by a ten-foot-tall wood palisade with four guard towers at each corner. In a one hundred feet radius around the outpost, all trees had been cut short in order to enhance the sentries field of vision. Luckily for him, George had brought a field-glass. He climbed to the tallest tree around and then brought the field-glass to his right eye. It gave him a clear sight of the guard towers. A strange feeling of disquiet slowly took hold of George as he looked and looked at the towers in search of sentries. After a few minutes, he had to admit the truth: there were none. It seemed the deserter had not entirely lied. George then studied the wall but did not see any sign of battle. Maybe the Vos had turned overconfident and taken this promised land for granted. If that was the case, they would regret it soon enough... George decided to wait for the night.

As the night covered the sky he approached one of the corners of the outpost. He took a few breaths and focused on the task ahead. Then he climbed the wall and reached the top after a few pushes. He jumped to the guard tower and started the ascension, hidden by shadows and darkness. At the top of the tower, he gave a good look at the unveiled outpost. He saw two dozen wooden structures of various shapes and builds. The Vos had taken no time to claim their new home and build a small tow of their own. If the walls have been devoid of life, that was not the case with the town. He saw a few Vos wander here and there, civilians and soldiers alike. No great numbers but it was night so nothing unusual about that. However, there was no semblance of patrols or orders. The soldiers blended with the civilians, some of them did not even carry their full set of weapons. George was surprised by this carelessness. The moon and the stars moved in the sky and gave way to a scorching sun. As day shone upon the outpost, life came out of the houses and barracks as the Vos wandered about they daily activities. George stayed in the tower for a while, observing them. Nothing stood out except for a strange lack of sound. The Vos were eerily silent. George discarded this strange mood as a portent of the upcoming doom that would befall his enemies.The day confirmed his observation about the Vos lack of vigilance. He also noticed that they were less numerous than what the size of the outpost suggested. A few eyes turned to the tower and George decided not to push his luck too far and went back to the fleet.

·

The meeting had lasted for much of the night as Constable Geralt, commander of the Mercian fleet, listened to each scout's finding one after the other. It seemed to last for an eternity to George as he reflected on his exploration.

"Your report George?" asked the Captain.

George shook his head and gave a summary of his findings. He omitted the deserter nonsensical mumbling.

"Marvelous." said Captain with a large grin. "Mark me gentlemen. We will take the new land from the Vos and built a New Mercia from its ground. Rest for today. We will move at dusk."

George had trouble finding sleep and spent most of the day talking with the other scouts. He gathered that the Vos had a dozen outposts in the new world. In some of them, they had commingled with what appeared to be the local population of the new world: a bunch of not very threatening savages armed with weapons made of wood, stones, and bones.

When dusk came, George led the troops of Mercia through the jungle. This night, the soldiers of Mercia donned the mask of death and savagery as they stormed the walls of the Vos outpost. The Vos did not even put up a fight as they were slaughtered like lambs. The savages were given Mercian "mercy" and were put in shackles to work in the fields. George did not revel in this victory. It had been server on a silver platter for no logical reason.

For a few weeks, it seemed that George was mistaken in his worries. The Mercians settled in their new colony and put the locals to work. It turned out that the Sals, as they liked to call themselves, were quick to pick-up the Mercian tongue. George himself owned a few Sals. He had to give them names since they lacked any sense of individuality. George had them working on his newly-possessed farm and he liked to inspect their work once in a while.

"You did a good job there Monday. Continue and we may have a talk about giving you more freedom of movement inside of the farm." said George.

"Thanks, my lord. You Mercians are really better than the Vos when it comes to farming... and war of course. We are really blessed to learn from you. By the way, I really like your hat sir." said Monday in a honeyed voice.

George was surprised by the linguistic mastery of Monday. It had only been a little more than one month. "Well, one day, you may have it as a reward.", he said in a voice that he hoped sounded strong and commanding.

Time went by and George found himself more and more invested in the running of his lands. The Sals impressed him with their dedication, their ability to pick up new skills and techniques, and their strong sense of discipline. They did not argue between themselves. In fact, they rarely talk if ever. At first, George took it as a sign of respect but with time he found it more and more disconcerting. He tried to engage in conversations with some of them and they were quite receptive to talk with him. However, he noticed something weird. They all talked in the same way and they seemed to share the same opinion on everything.

•

A few weeks later, a fair was organized in the capital city of New Mercia, called Geralton in honor of the Constable. When George arrived, he was impressed by the advanced state of the new city. It mixed Vos and Mercian architecture and blended gracefully with the surrounding environment, using oak trees as points of structure for some of its buildings. The city was eerily quiet despite the vast number of Sals and Mercians selling goods. He had expected more noise from merchants and farmers as they tried to draw crowds to their stall and outsold each other. On the contrary, People did not try to barter at all. They just traded goods peacefully without a word exchanged. It was as if the Mercians had turned into Sals. George chased this discomforting thought from his mind and tried to find some of this old friends. It turned out they were not very receptive to talk about the time before the landing. Their interest focused on expanding New Mercia, trading goods and making the kingdom more prosperous. Something was very wrong, but what?

As he was going to leave the fair, George crossed Constable Geralt on the street. The Constable was without an escort, among the crowd. He waved at George, grinned and said: "Good to see you, George. I've heard your farm is growing well. That's very good. We want this colony to expand more and more. By the way I've never told you but your really have a nice hat. Cocked-hat they call it, isn't it?"

A wave of unease washed over George's inside as he tried to smile. For a moment, it seemed that the crowd was watching him and grinning in perfect synchronization with the Constable. The words of the deserter came back to him: *"They're all dead inside. They all belong to him...".* George tried to stay as still as possible and replied in his best non-shaking voice: "You're honoring me sir. My only desire is to make new Mercia greater and greater.". George saluted and went his way. Afterwhile, he told his Salts to wait for him at the east exit of town. He went to the west exit and waited until he was outside of sight to run as fast as possible. New Mercia was lost. The new land was cursed. But there was still hope. He could reach the coast, board a ship, and warn the homeland.

As he reached the coast, George saw that the Mercian fleet was in flames. Surrounded it, a vast fleet of ships, arboring the black and gold flag of the Teuton Empire. He decided to try his chance and lighted a torch. Before he could wave it, he felt a hard push and stumbled to the ground. He looked up and saw Constable Geralt and a vast number of Mercians, Sals and Voss. As the Constable bent to take Geralt hat and put it on his head, he looked at the Teuton fleet and said with a carnivorous smile: "Oh a new colony..."

Author's Note

I planned it to be longer and had to make it shorter. As you will notice, it should have been more subtle and slower and less abrupt. Hope you still enjoy it and don't get too confused.

EIGHTEEN YEARS

Brandon Butler

Persisting in a dimensional state isn't as difficult as it sounds. It's not difficult at all, really, since you don't have to do anything but exist. But when you're personally there and not part of some capsule or interstellar vessel (put a pin on that one, we'll be coming back to it) you don't experience things like regular. You don't see, hear or smell, you don't process thought quite the same. You're literally spread out between realities, after all, and that can leave you feeling a bit out of touch.

So that said, I had what resembled a conversation somewhere beyond the limits of perception where words and ideas and feelings are more important than a place or time of day.

Hello, something said to me. Upon reflection, its tone sounded pretty curious.

Hey, I said back, except I wasn't using words. I was more thinking it all, and for all I knew it took half a second or entire months to say.

What are you doing here?

Waiting. Or sleeping, sort of. What are you doing here?

I live here.

Well, this was awkward. Protocols on dimensional travel never said anything about beings living in the other slices of reality that we used to get from one galactic neighborhood to the next. Of course whatever the Aggregate Governments were saying was the furthest thing from my mind since right then I didn't really have one. *Oh,* I said. *Sorry. I won't be here long. I'm just visiting.*

You have travelled here?
Sort of. More passing through.
Why?
It's my job.
What is a 'job'?

So straight away I knew this was going to take a while, but I didn't really have anything else to do. After explaining the particulars of economics and occupation to the satisfaction of my new friend, he asked, *What is your job?*

I'm a Captain. Sub-Captain Lovel.

Sub-Captain?

Yeah. Sort of a backup Captain provided by our mission backers. Done this a few times now. I'm only here on an as-needed basis if the Captain screws up or goes AWOL or something. Heck, even the Captain's out here, somewhere. The ship's just flying itself right now. You know how these things go.

No. I do not know how these things go.

Right, so this guy was gonna be one of those literal types. How long was he going to stick around? This trip was getting off to a great start. *Thing is, I'm not a real Captain,* I said, *not how most people think. Oh, I know how the basics and where everything goes, but most people who think 'ship' and 'crew' follow it up by thinking 'military'. I'm not that. Now, the actual Captain? He really is one of those offshoot types that's gone private sector. Maybe a couple of the other crew too. But most of us are civilian through and through, like the old Merchant Marines.* I paused. *Please don't ask me about that.*

It seemed to be taking it all in. I hadn't even mentioned Earth yet, but we'd be here all day if I got into that. Or whatever unit of measurement made most sense in this ether of existence. Then finally it said, *Will they need you?*

Haven't needed me yet, I replied. If I could grin out here, I would have flashed it one. *Easy times, easy money. Just sit back, close your eyes and cruise the stars.*

•

I was pulled together from a billion directions, remade anew in my own image, uncertain on when exactly I'd started to think again in the regular fashion. The first thing I really did remember was Captain Wilson staring at me in the Dimension Chamber, looking serious. He looked about to speak but was interrupted before he could begin by a gentle voice that filled the room. "PROCESS COMPLETE. SUBJECT RE-INITIALIZED."

Wilson shot an ugly glance up toward the ceiling. "Lovel," he said, "there's a problem."

"Oh," I said back with a cough, taking a moment to get my bearings. I looked down. "Could I get a set of clothes?"

"No time," replied Wilson, and threw me the towel he carried over an arm. It was long, and I tied it around my waste. He indicated for me to follow. "We've abandoned the landing site."

"Abandoned? Why?"

"Wasn't my decision."

We walked out into the empty metal hallways of *Santa Nina*, almost nobody around. I spotted a dirty plate on one of the side tables in a nearby alcove so I knew some of the other guys had to be up and around, somewhere. I didn't really know very many of them that well though, so in a way it didn't matter too much. "So we're just… not going to the planet?"

"You got it. It's occupied."

Occupied? Really? I'd thought our backers were diligent about this stuff. I mean, taking people from one planet to the next was no small thing. You had to think about families, communities, interpersonal relationships, the whole bit. I knew there was a whole small town from the south side of Mars on here somewhere. "Occupied by who?"

"Other people."

I swung around in front of him. He was a big guy, only a little older than me, late thirties. He had one of those thick mustaches and hints of a neck tattoo below the collar, probably from his days in the navy. He didn't flaunt it much though. He was ok like that. "Wait, there's *humans* there? Doesn't that defeat the purpose?"

He took a step around me, pretty determined to get us where he was headed. "That's what the records say. It all happened when I was out. Mission plan dictates I only be brought out if there's more than the standard five course deviations and we only logged two minor ones on our way there. The other three happened around the same time we diverted course from our second destination."

He was pulling away. I hurried my pace to keep a few steps behind, tightening the towel around my waist. "*Second* destination? What was wrong with the first?"

"Occupied. Like I said."

"But it's a whole *planet*. There's no reason we can't touch down anyway."

"Yes. I know that. You know that. But our handy mission software programmed by those smart boys with their big brains apparently don't know that. Or they overthought it."

I asked him more questions – where we were diverted to, where we were headed now – and he answered each one patiently, not looking back. After we'd taken the lift I took a moment to start thinking in the here and now and realized we were almost at the bridge.

I walked up beside Wilson. "You know," he said, "I was thinking I should apologize."

"For what?"

He didn't respond, just took the last few steps as the doors opened to a wide hexagonal room with edges so straight they looked cut from the inside of a diamond. A few more of the crew were here, skeleton staff all of them. The second mate and a couple lieutenants. One was a woman… Gloria something, I think, but she was polite enough to avert her gaze from the obvious. Besides those three, I spotted one other face I recognized: Miles, the engineer, a Brit by way of Trinidad or Guyana or somewhere around the south Caribbean. He looked up at me, grinned and gave a little two-fingered salute.

I ignored him, walking around the end of the bridge as Wilson strode into the center. Almost everything here was interactive, with screens along the walls and holograms ready to fill any necessary space. Only the chairs and doors were pretty much meant to function exactly as you saw them. Right now the place was lit in blue and green, shimmering lights from opposing corners in the floor and ceiling.

"Any luck?" Wilson asked the crew.

Miles gave a little laugh. "What, did you think we were going to crack the whole thing while you were gone?"

"That's not what I asked."

Miles took a cigarette from his pocket. You weren't supposed to smoke in here but he was the kinda guy who'd like to see you come over and tell him that. "No. Nav's not responding." He looked over at me, getting the hint to bring me into the loop. "Nothing today, nothing yesterday, nothing for the whole week we've been up."

"You mean it's broken?" I asked.

He was in the midst of his drag so he took a while to respond. "No, sorry, I mean it is responding, it's just not really paying us any attention. Not where navigation is concerned. I can't boot it off course, can't turn us around…" he adjusted the polite pair of glasses he wore over his nose. "I could speed us up, I think, or slow us down if it wouldn't make things worse. But otherwise?" Miles shook his head.

I tried to remember what he was saying. They suspended colonists in inert (supposedly) pocket dimensions but phasing in and out of existence was par for the course in space travel too. Only difference was you were doing it in a shared physical environment like the *Santa Nina* instead of experiencing it personally. Dimensional shifting was the hot new thing for the past couple generations so you saw it crop up all over now.

"That's what I thought. All right, clear the bridge," Wilson said. "I need to explain a few things captain-to-captain."

They did as he bid, although I caught the little eye-roll from Miles as he left. Once they were gone, I said, "are you really sure I can't just go and get some clothes?"

"In a bit. Look Lovel, we've done a couple of these stints now. The trips were all shorter, not that it matters… but I know we don't know each other very well."

I shrugged. "You're the day shift," I said. "I'm the no-shift."

"Right," he said. "So really you're up to speed at this point. We've got a computer whose mind we can't seem to change on where we're headed, and it's one big goddamn problem." He headed over to the Captain's chair, picked up a tablet lying in the seat and dropped it again. "I've been reading up on the team that put it together and… not sure if this is connected… but there seems to be a history of gambling with the programmers and AI helping subroutines. Looks like a lot of them were involved with Game Theory or Risk Management and I wouldn't be surprised if we're stuck with a program guaranteed to choose the most ambitious, most striving path for the best possible choice of world that our backers can make money on. I don't know that, but I've got a gut feeling and my gut feelings are the most important things I've ever learned to trust."

"Sounds reasonable," I said, with no idea if it was. "But why did you wake me? Need an extra pair of hands?"

"Certainly," Wilson said, walking over to the far side of the bridge. There was a hologram button-panel hovering near the wall on that side. "But also to apologize. We never really got to know one another and that seems a bit unfair."

I gave a nervous chuckle, feeling the goosebumps form along my back. It was getting a little cool in here. "You're in a tight spot."

"Sort of." Wilson punched in a code on the keypad. A door slid open on the wall that hadn't seemed to be there before. I remember this coming up in orienteering and that it went somewhere but I was drawing a blank on what it was. Wilson turned around. "I thought it might be a good time to confess something. I'm not military, not really. I used to be, yeah, but that was a long time ago and I was actually court-marshalled out of the service. Dereliction of duty."

"Oh, I'm… sorry to hear that?"

"No need. I was guilty as charged. I actually had a second career as a mercenary. This was meant to be my peacetime gig and it's gotten me about as far as care to take it. So I should apologize."

"Why?"

"Because we're in the middle of dimensional travel, and all the escape pods are incapable of independently shifting reality. Except one."

Then Wilson took a single step backward into the doorway, pressed a button somewhere on the inside, and the door slid back shut.

I raced over to the door, tried pressing on the hologram pad but nothing was giving and I couldn't remember what the code had been. Pounding on the wall, I cried out to summon the crew and within minutes they'd returned. I called up the external cameras and above our heads a red expanse opened up with curving lines of black and green, like an interstellar borealis. I wasn't sure which dimension this was, but nothing outside resembled anything from our reality. I saw the sleek edges of the *Santa Nina* as a tiny triangular vessel spat off from the edge and out into the unknown, speeding away.

"What happened?" asked Gloria. The timbre of her voice was high, skirting the edge of panic. "Did we stop the ship?"

Miles knew right away. "The Captain bailed," he said. His cigarette hung limp from his lips. "Damn. Wish I had thought of that."

•

Memories of the conversation came in parcels. The longer I stayed awake, the more I remembered of what happened in stasis.

Why did you choose this? It had asked me.

Not really sure, I said. *I've travelled between the colonies for years and years. The local ones, I mean, not these deep-space adventures. Skipping between this and that port, taking work as you find it. Employment comes easier the further you get from Earth. Do it long enough and you make a name for yourself. This just seemed a logical extension.*

So you enjoy it.

I enjoy a lot of things. Girls, music, a good Merlot… this will do.

It was quiet for a while, although what I mean by quiet and what I mean by a while isn't exactly right. I remember noise like a strange rushing of wind and a throbbing pulse and, as for the gap in time, I'm not sure of the sequence in anything either of us said. What came before may have come after, and vice versa. But at some point we stopped communicating and started up again, so my description will have to serve.

What are you? I asked it.

You have something I do not, Sub-Captain Lovel. A name. My people have no such designations. But we travel now between dimensions. It is a recent development.

It's the hot new thing, I said.

Indeed. We are explorers. We come and go and return home as we will. We have never met anyone such as you. We have never met anyone, in fact, beyond ourselves. Had we encountered one another in most dimensions we would be unable to communicate; we do not possess mouths as you understand them. But you interest me. Your dimension sounds so tangible and incredible. And this thing you mention… what was it, I cannot…

Colony? I asked. I try to help out when I can.

Yes. Colony. To stay in a place other than where you are from. I have never heard of this idea. The concept is no doubt foreign to our species. Or perhaps suggested once or twice like so many discarded thoughts but long ago forgotten.

It's all we're about anymore, I told it. *Leave our species in one place long enough, it gets harder for the average person to stay after a few hundred years. Lack of social mobility and all that. I can't even stand the homeworld any more. Earth. Bunch of stuck up pricks.*

It sounds terrible, the presence said. *Tell me.*

•

Two days later we gathered everyone we could that was up and moving around the *Santa Nina*. Miles, the Gloria chick, second mate guy, and something like another fifteen men and women. Essential personnel filling various roles around the ship, awakened along with Wilson. Only a couple of them were actual colonists bound for wherever we wound up going. Most of us were space and dimensional regulars with no regular port of call that we could call home.

"Okay people," I said, raising a hand for silence after we'd been gathered for a good ten minutes. "Hi there, Sub-Captain Lovel. Looks like I'm in charge. Unless anyone else wants…"

They all gave me a weird look after that. Right. Wrong thing to say.

I clapped my hands together. "Well it seems we're caught in a bind. For anyone who doesn't know, the Captain left. Straight up took off. He took the only functional escape pod that can travel between dimensions and thanks to our nav computer, there's no way to cut our trip short." I looked over at the Engineer. "Miles, you had something you wanted to say?"

Miles stood up. Another cigarette was in his mouth and I pretty much hadn't seen him without one since waking. He scratched at the brown skin of his acne-scarred cheek before he began. "Ok so, near as I can figure we've been in space for about three or four years Earth-time given time dilation. There were some records of the auto-encounter the *Santa Nina* made near to our original stop before it started pulling us back into our roles, and it looks like there's been developments since we began the journey. Do all of you know how dimensional travel works?"

He looked around at us. Nobody said anything. I certainly

didn't.

"Do *any* of you know how it works?"

Silence.

Miles took in a long breath. "Okay, so… let's make this easy… there's these, let's call them travel points between dimensions. They're not stationary or anything, it's just the point at which a given navigation course decides it's going to enter another dimension. There's a corresponding point for where your given ship is going to exit out of the same dimension and back into the lovely Milky Way. In our reality, the distance between these two points is very, very far apart, but here it's much shorter. So it works like taking a galactic shortcut: you physically travel only a fraction of the distance that you end up traversing."

There was a long moment of silence. The smoke from Miles cigarette could be seen floating around the overhead lamps, creating a hell of an atmosphere around the table. "That's pretty cool," I said. The rest of the crew nodded in agreement. One started to applaud, but got the hint after a few claps.

Miles bent his head down, shooting me a look over the rim of his glasses. "The tech's been on the books for decades. Anyway, it seems one of our competitor organizations developed some upgraded ships not long after we left. More to the point, they discovered a better dimension with closer travel points. So they're completely outclassing our stuff and getting ahead of us at every turn. I wouldn't be surprised if our parent company's out of business."

"That doesn't explain why we can't land," I said.

"It's the competition," Miles said. "Part of the money in this is exclusivity rights. Looks like the nav computer's just auto-designed to say 'fuck that' and pick a new destination. Guess they didn't figure on us getting out-dimensioned by an entire generation of colony vessels. Good thing fuel out here isn't too much of a worry."

Gloria raised a hand. I pointed to her. "So what do we do?"

I sat up. I'd talked this over a little with Miles. "Well we can ride out the current destination and hope the competition just doesn't arrive there yet," I said, "or we try to stop the ship."

Gloria pushed her heavy bangs out of the way. She wore a leather jacket over her uniform. Can you believe it? I'm not an expert or anything but did she realize it wasn't 30 years ago? Time dilation just doesn't work that way. "Isn't that dangerous?" she asked.

"Could be. But we're considering how it could be done. Thought we should put it to a vote. Only fair right?" I stood up, looking them all over, trying my best for once to look authoritative. "All right. Everyone in favor of stopping the ship?"

Miles raised his hand. A few of the others did as well. I made a quick count. Five.

I nodded. "Ok, all for riding this out?"

I raised my hand with the rest of the crew except Gloria. I looked at her. "This *all* sucks," she said.

"Ok, so that's five for stopping, nine for riding it out, and one abstention."

Miles leaned forward. "There's five thousand lives on this ship you're making this decision for, you know."

I sighed. It wasn't like he didn't have a point. "Sorry Miles," I said, "but-"

The polite, booming voice resonated above our heads. "UPDATE. UPDATE. COURSE CORRECTION. NEW DESTINATION REQUIREMENTS. CALCULATING..."

I turned to Miles. "What's it doing?"

"Looking for a new destination. What, you can't hear?"

"Why is it looking? What's wrong with the old one?"

Miles shrugged. "Our competitors strike again."

"We're in a whole other dimension! How's it gonna know?"

"It's not like people stopped coming through here," Miles said. "There's flight paths criss-crossing all over this dimensional sector. Other ships jump in, auto-link to ours to coordinate long distance with latest galactic information and..."

The booming voice returned. "COURSE CORRECTION COMPLETE. PLANET DETECTED AND ACQUIRED. NEW DESTINATION REGULUS XIX ALPHA. ADDITIONAL TIME ADDED TO ROUTE: FOURTEEN YEARS."

The crew started murmuring amongst themselves. Gloria gave a cry and hung her head so low her forehead came to rest against the table.

"All right," I said so everyone could hear. "We're stopping this ship."

•

I was down in one of the lower access tunnels, back chafing against a bulkhead. "Do you see it?" Miles asked from speakers all around me.

I looked up and over, adjusting the light resting atop my shoulder. I fixed my eyes on the energy panel and reached up, flipping it open and keying in the code for administrative access. I'd reviewed all the necessary codes and passwords since Wilson had left us holding the intergalactic bag. I toggled the safety off the main switch and set it to active position before adjusting the camera that sat just below the light. "All set."

"Oh yeah, uh…" Miles trailed off. Must have been looking over what I'd done. "Yeah, that's right. You've done this before."

"Something like it," I said. "Near Jupiter. Are you sure the colonists will be ok?"

"They've got the entire reserve system," he said. "It's a totally independent backup just for them. They'll only have to worry if we can't get main power back online."

"Which we can totally do."

A long pause. "That's the hope," he said. "You sure you don't want to hail another ship?"

I sighed. We'd been trying for days. No luck. There had to be other vessels out there still traversing this obsolete dimension, but probably from other companies and without orders to bother responding on any conscious level. Crews likely asleep with AIs running standard operating non-interference procedures. "No," I said, "We'll try this. I'll give the order. All right, everybody on the channel check in and stand by." I listened as the rest of the crew read off their position and status from various parts of the ship. I spared myself a little grin. Each one of them reporting to me. I'd done it freelance here and there in the past, but I'd forgotten how being in charge of a crew held its little moments.

The last one sounded off. I keyed in the comm, grabbing the open handle. "All right. Miles? Ashenfort? You ready on the auxiliary switches? On my mark. Three, two, one, go!" I rotated the thing as hard as I could to the right, resting it in a horizontal position. There was a distant, descending drone. Everything went dark.

Ashenfort's voice over the line. "Did it work?"

And then a crash, with Gloria shouting, "No, no, no, no! Turn it back on!"

"What's wrong?"

"Coolant leak! Turn it back on! We've got a coolant leak in-" a burst of static before she cut off.

I started twisting the handle back the other way. "Miles!"

"On it."

Pulling the handle back upright, I waited. The low static hiss still hung upon the air. Finally, the light returned. Things seemed to be coming back up. "Gloria?" I said into the comm. "Gloria?"

Miles came back on the line. "Half of aft twelve deck just sealed," he said. "Her station. Not responding."

I sat back, hand trembling. I wiped sweat from my face where none had been moments ago. Gloria – I'd never learned her last name. I'd known her face for quite a while, we'd run just as many trips together as Wilson, maybe more, but I never gave much her much thought beyond what she presented to the world. "Jesus," I said. "Ashenfort get down there, see what you can do. How's the rest looking? Did it work?"

Nobody said anything. And then, the voice, only too familiar now: "UPDATE. UPDATE. POWER DISRUPTION. COURSE CORRECTION. NEW DESTINATION REGULUS XIX ALPHA. ADDITIONAL TIME ADDED TO ROUTE: FOURTEEN YEARS."

I hung my head low, hearing the computer's voice echo through the tunnel but hearing only what mattered. "FOURTEEN YEARS… FOURTEEN YEARS… FOURTEEN YEARS…"

•

Alone in the Captain's quarters. They were mostly empty, Wilson hadn't spent any time over the week he'd been awake making himself at home. It was pretty routine for this room never to be used. Would probably make more sense as a storage closet. But then, with me here, that's pretty much exactly what it was. I took another drink of brandy straight from the bottle.

It had taken another day to get anyone into aft twelve deck and another three to clean it out. It had been pretty much how you'd expect. But no coolant leak. Gloria had been able to shut that down before breathing too much of the stuff into her system. I swayed the bottle in my hand, looking out a window at the foreign red reality beyond.

I wasn't sure what to do with her body. Would a service classify as a burial at sea, abandoning her remains out here? Was that what she would have even wanted?

I didn't know.

I was still staring out that window when I heard something behind me. I turned around.

A grey… thing was there. Long and thin and floating, it looked like a staff or snake fully extended top to bottom, no winding of its body, with a head bent down and no eyes. Just a shifting pattern there, tiny dots of black growing and disappearing in lines across its surface. Its skin seemed cloudy; opaque, but as if I could pass my hand through it.

I fell off my chair.

Something fell to the ground before it. I looked over. It was round and metallic but with a port that looked familiar. Looked like it would fit into a normal LB7 adapter. I looked up at the thing, but it didn't move. I almost said something, but kept silent.

We stayed like that for a long time. Finally I got up and dared to get closer, snatching the device from the floor. It didn't move. I got away as soon as I could and looked around for the right adapter. There was one atop the desk and I inserted the device into it.

"Hello Sub-Captain Lovell," a voice said.

I'd fully remembered it by then. "Hello," I said back.

"I understand you have problems."

"You could say that. How did you know?"

"The same way, by extrapolation, that I now know your language in its proper form. I have taken pieces and memories from my encounters and taken them for study in a custom dimension where time flows differently. I created that communication device there, to measure my gaseous releases in some form of your language. It has been, as I experience time now on this vessel, long since we have spoken. Approaching perhaps twenty of your Earth years."

"Neat," I said flatly. He seemed proud of that explanation.

"Are you in need of assistance?"

I paused. Could this thing really be of help? "Yes," I said. "Yes I am. We are."

"I surmised as much. I am in your debt Sub-Captain, all of my people are. Without you we would be stuck in old ways of thinking. Enthralling how chance encounters often change the course of history. I have studied the problem of your ship. I think we may be able to draw you back into your parent reality."

I could have kissed the thing if it didn't look so creepy. So instead I said, "That's good."

"It involves further shifting of realities. But because of how you entered this place and the laws and physics of this realm, I can only ferry you to your intended destination. What you know as Regulus XIX Alpha."

"That's what the colonists are here for."

"Good. The experience should be close to instantaneous. Shall I do this for you, then?"

I sat down into the chair behind the desk tilting my head back, letting the cool air conditioning of the room waft over me. Thank God. And if this happened to be God, alien deity before me on loan from heaven, thank It. "Yes," I said. "Yes, please do."

"Very W-"

It cut off. I blacked out completely.

When I came to, my head was on the desk. So was the bottle of brandy, my hand wrapped around it. The creature was still there. "It is done," it said.

I turned around. Safe and familiar stars twinkled back, with a green planet below. I bent forward, holding my face in my hands. A comm keyed in, Miles voice sounding bewildered and excited, but I cut it off. No offense Miles, I just need to be alone right now. I stood, walked over to the window and looked down at the planet. Our orbit favored its dark side, a thick colorful crescent of maroon land and emerald ocean set between solar shadow and the light of a bright orange sun. I looked down into the fathomless depths of night that lay below. "Home at last," I said, permitting myself a chuckle. "For now."

"Do you like it?" the creature asked. "More than Earth?"

I didn't move from the window. "Already? Possibly. Probably. It's been a long time since I've been back. Maybe I'll take a nice long trip there once I get the last of my pay, see how it stacks up to what's going on out here. Maybe I'm too tough on the old girl. Maybe things have changed."

"They have," said the creature. "It is gone."

I turned around, looking into its strange black lines of dots. "What's gone?"

"Earth. Not the place, but the people. We have taken them and their structures from the planet for study. We wish to know more of your first colony and how it was done. You shall find the ecosystem quite ready for re-habitation."

I laughed. The thing was putting me on, now. Besides I wasn't sure it was getting its terminology right. "It's the homeworld," I said, "not a colony. I wouldn't bother with them. I'm pretty sure they're fine where they are."

Quiet. It did not speak to me, nor I to it. "Goodbye, Sub-Captain," it finally said, "our debt is paid." And then it faded from existence before I could say another word.

I walked over to the desk. I pulled the device from the adapter and stood where the creature had been. Nothing. As if it had never been here. I was already forgetting how it looked, what it had sounded like.

And then, I felt the floor shift beneath me, ever so slightly. I turned to the window and saw the planet falling out of view. We were turning around. I raced around the desk and when I gripped my fingers back upon the window ledge I now spotted the dim lights of what must have been a fresh, brave new colony dotting the edge of the planetary horizon where I'd noticed none before, its proud and distant inhabitants just now settling themselves for dusk. I thought of the escape pods, now functional while we remained in our own galaxy, and how far I'd have to go to reach them. And then of the five thousand men, women and children caught between realities that couldn't possibly make it in time.

The voice of the computer descended, nesting within my ears, booming and informative and so, so polite: "UPDATE. UPDATE. COURSE CORRECTION. NEW DESTINATION REQUIREMENTS. PLANET DETECTED AND ACQUIRED. NEW DESTINATION -- EARTH. ADDITIONAL TIME ADDED TO ROUTE: EIGHTEEN YEARS… EIGHTEEN

Brandon Butler

YEARS… EIGHTEEN YEARS…"

THE ANTEDILUVIAN WORLD

Jayant Avva

Timaeus Excerpt 1

"For it is related in our records how once upon a time your State stayed the course of a mighty host, which, starting from a distant point in the Atlantic ocean, was insolently advancing to attack the whole of Europe, and Asia to boot. For the ocean there was at that time navigable; for in front of the mouth which you Greeks call, as you say, 'the pillars of Heracles,' there lay an island which was larger than Libya and Asia together; and it was possible for the travelers of that time to cross from it to the other islands, and from the islands to the whole of the continent over against them which encompasses that veritable ocean. For all that we have here, lying within the mouth of which we speak, is evidently a haven having a narrow entrance; but that yonder is a real ocean, and the land surrounding it may most rightly be called, in the fullest and truest sense, a continent. Now in this island of Atlantis there existed a confederation of kings, of great and marvelous power, which held sway over all the island, and over many other islands also and parts of the continent."

Timaeus Excerpt 2

"But afterwards there occurred violent earthquakes and floods; and in a single day and night of misfortune all your warlike men in a body sank into the earth, and the island of Atlantis in like manner disappeared in the depths of the sea. For which reason the sea in those parts is impassable and impenetrable, because there is a shoal of mud in the way; and this was caused by the subsidence of the island."

-Plato, Timaeus, 360 BCE (Translated by Benjamin Jowett).

1. The Search

1940 CE.

The rain forest has a very diverse audio spectrum. Keith closed his eyes. Someone with their eyes closed would hear every emotion represented in these sounds. The violent sounds of carnivores tearing into their prey could be discerned if you were near watering holes. In the right season, you could hear the passion of the throes of the 'little death' of mating throngs. The human imagination would add a healthy dose of the spook factor to every nocturnal sound. The visuals would be every bit as diverse an array, as would the rich and textured scents and smells that lingered in the forest air.

Keith's imagination was perhaps just as neurotic as your average human being, and it was night when he found himself in the African forest. He didn't know where he was. It was clear enough that he was losing his grip on reality. He could barely remember how cities looked anymore. The all consuming search had in fact consumed most of all he owned, except for his mind - and now that seemed to be slipping.

The colony was supposed to be somewhere in the heart of the grand Congo. One single colony of that grand sunken continent that some supposed was mythical - Atlantis. Atlantis! It was all the rage because of how fascinating the legend was, and yet there were plenty of skeptics. There was one section of the archaeological community who were beginning wield a lot of power, and these were the skeptics who put a hold on the flow of monies to finance anything related to Atlantis. An academic interest in Atlantis was a great way to become the laughing stock of your university faculty. This increasingly influential section said that Plato was being figurative when he mentioned the grand continent in his dialogues Timaeus and Critias.

Keith felt it in his bones when he first viewed the map, and heard the tale of strange people with advanced technology who called the heart of the dark continent their home. The tale, now a legend, spoke of these strange people, who were a mixture of races, who spoke of their home continent. They spoke of a place larger than Asia in the Atlantic Ocean. They spoke of strange flying vehicles and technology that sounded like magic to Keith's mind.

Human beings flying in contraptions. What a strange and fantastic thought indeed! Human beings wielding strange weapons and speaking a language that was both ancient and modern when viewed through different prisms.

Keith had started out with a whole safari, which included two of his partners and financiers, and a whole team of native Congolese who carried the heavy stuff, and who knew the smells, sounds and sights of this forest. The lion attack marked the turning point for what appeared to be a fairly uneventful safari. One fine afternoon, while the safari set up their boma near a watering hole, they noticed that one of the financiers was missing. They discovered a half eaten mangled carcass a few hours later, with certain indications that told the natives that it was a lion that had done the damage. The other financier took half the safari and turned right around and left. That left Keith and his Congolese porters and guides with half the supplies.

They lost a porter the next day, and but this time they heard his heartrending cry. They never found his whole body, but the other porters discovered his foot after half a day of scouting. This spelled the end for their participation.

"The spirits of the jungle are angry with us," they told him. "They want us to turn back."

They delivered an ultimatum to Keith.

"Come back with us, or go on ahead by yourself!"

Keith tried all the tricks of cajoling and bullying that he could think of, but nothing worked. They were turning around. This deep into jungle, and the ever present dangers, were enough to scare even these hardened denizens of the forest. Keith refused to turn around. Perhaps it was a mental affliction of some kind. Perhaps it was something else. Something inside him urged him on.

If I am going to die, then I may as well die in an interesting way.

That sounded like something whose ticket has already been checked would say. But he felt it in his bones. He felt the colony he was searching for. He prayed he wasn't being foolish, like someone chasing the horizon and trying to capture it.

One leather water bottle that was mostly empty, and a piece of a buffalo shank for sustenance - these were what was left of the meager possessions that the Congolese had left him with. It was evening, and Keith kept trudging on, perhaps like a fool. Leopards and lots of other predators hunted at night, and he wouldn't be able to see his own feet in the unnerving darkness of the forest night. Perhaps he should find himself safe in the branches of a tree somewhere. Perhaps. But there was a voice within him that whispered about the legend, and the voice had only gotten stronger as his physical form progressively lost vigor. He decided to use what little daylight was left to keep moving towards what appeared to be the correct direction.

He felt something inside him tingling. He was being watched. He felt a tug in his solar plexus that reminded him of just keen and visceral fear can be. Keith started making a beeline for the tree that was nearest him, which in itself looked like it would be quite a challenge to scale. He never made it. He felt a heavy blow to the back of his head, which immediately ushered in the pitch blackness of unconsciousness.

2. The Colony

When he awoke, his first sensation was that of a dull ache in his head. He tried to move and noticed that he could move only so much. He had been laid on a long piece of furniture that was part bed, part divan. His eyes adjusted to the light, and he saw that he was next to a wall. The wall was a revelation. It showed a scene of war. On one side, there were people who were painted as being olive skinned and dressed in what could be ancient Hellenic garbs, seated in chariots or standing on foot. On the other side were their opponents, people who had many hues to their skin, and who were seated in bejeweled flying vehicles that were depicted as being sophisticated and armed to the teeth. He saw strange scripts on the wall, that were seemingly naming different objects in the scene.

He didn't know what to make of it. The script reminded him of the Sanskrit script - Devanagari as it was called in Sanskrit. He wasn't an Indologist or an expert in it, so he had no way of saying what it said. He heard a slight sound behind him, and was joined by a tall man who was light skinned and sported a long, well groomed beard, and short, white hair. The man was dressed in what looked like a Japanese kimono that had a bare design and looked very comfortable. Wise sky blue eyes met his own, indicating no fear and no hostility.

"Hello," the stranger said. "You've had quite the journey."

"Praise the Lord! You speak English!" Keith said.

The man nodded. He had an accent that was very difficult to pinpoint. Nondescript was the word that came to mind.

"I do, but let's talk about you first," he said. "Who are you, and why are you here?"

"My name is Keith Annable, and I have come in search of the last colony of Atlantis."

The man vouchsafed no response.

"Does the name Atlantis mean anything to you?" Keith asked.

The man looked at him, and his eyes were sad.

"You want to share your knowledge with others from your civilization, I suppose," he said. "I'll tell you for a fact that you cannot leave here. We keep to ourselves for several excellent reasons."

Keith nodded. He had contemplated this possibility. There was no point arguing about it, given his position. The man hadn't answered his question, but there was tacit admission in his talk about Keith's knowledge.

May as well have an interesting time.

"I am curious - why am I not hungry?" Keith half asked, half said to himself.

"You were really weak, so we gave you nutrition while you were asleep," the man said. "Let me apologize for the blow to your head. One of our guards got over zealous."

Keith nodded, but his mind was racing. He had a hundred questions about their medical technology alone. How? How could they have fed him while he was asleep? What sort of marvelous advances in medicine had these people come up with? Why had he not felt a thing? Why were there no adverse after effects? But there were more immediate questions.

"Do you have a name?" he asked the man.

"Jata," the man said.

"Where am I?" he asked.

"You're under quarantine, and this is as much for your protection, as it is for us."

Keith understood somewhat, being familiar with more about the concept of a quarantine, having spent his life in contact with academic institutions.

"You will be confined to this room," Jata said, "within which we have created a sterile zone. Keep in mind that some of our native germs may not suit your constitution, and what you bear on your body may not suit ours."

"Then how is it that you can share this room with me?"

"I am protected by a field around me," Jata said, giving no further explanation.

The quarantine lasted a week. It was a week of rapid learning though. Keith met either with Jata or with Gala, a lady who appeared to be in her fifties, and was around Keith's height, and sported yellow-white hair. Her garments, like Jata's, were very simple garments with bare designs that reminded him of Japanese kimonos.

Between his two hosts, Keith learned a lot about their history. They were indeed an advanced civilization, who had access to technologies that were akin to magic to Keith. He questioned them about their flying machines, and learned that they did have flying machines aplenty. They called them their *Vimanas*, which, he was told, was the same as the Sanskrit word for a flying machine. They maintained an unbroken record of the last twenty thousand years, and they shared some tidbits with him.

9000 years before Critias (460 - 403 BCE), whom Plato had written about, there had indeed been a large continent that was the home of the ancestors of Jata and Gala and their kind. They spoke to Keith of a rapid series of natural disasters that had unfolded in their original homeland, which led to its ultimate destruction. They also told him about the violent conflicts that their ancestors had with ancient Hellenes. The archaeologist in Keith had goosebumps, as he began to understand that a lot of what had been the topic of heated debate in the archaeological community was actually very close to what Plato had written about.

The destruction of their homeland had been violent, and it had vanished beneath the waves in matter of days. Keith shared his knowledge of Plato and what the ancient Greeks thought of Atlantis, and his hosts agreed on many facets of the lore.

His hosts showed him a sequence of lifelike scenes that unfolded as though they were happening in his presence. There were no actors or people that entered his quarantine chamber, but to his eyes, three dimensional images danced and lived and fought and died around him. The soil of his imagination was further watered by seeing ancient Hellenes in garb that he had seen in ancient amphorae and rock paintings and other ancient Hellenic art forms. He saw these ancient peoples fighting the Atlanteans, pitting their primitive spears and swords and archery against light and firepower raining from flying chariots.

Entire fleets were shown being decimated by the hovering *Vimanas*, as they tore through the Hellenes' defenses again and again, in skirmish after skirmish, as part of a war that lasted for centuries. Centuries that had been lost to history.

Then he saw more peaceful scenes, as if his hosts were pacing the violence in order to give his constitution some respite. He saw grand halls filled with art and architecture that would have made the Renaissance masters' works look like the abject scribbles of children. He saw throngs of people dancing, and loving, and he saw every kind of sexual congress. He saw technology that raised many questions, but before he could move to ask them, he saw something else that captured his fancy. He saw aerial views of their cities, and gigantic statues that would have made the famed Colossus of Rhodes seem a dwarf. *Vimanas* patrolled the skies, offering the citizens protection from there.

Then they showed him one part of what had been the end for their continent. He saw people running while tall buildings collapsed on them. He saw lava breaking the earth's surface, and setting people on fire. He saw the beautiful halls that had filled him with wonder go up in flames, with scores of people trapped within. He heard the wailing of numberless people, and felt anguish course through his body. He was about to beg his hosts to stop, when the scenes of horror stopped.

He saw people flying in *Vimanas* away from a fiery and violent land, that shot out tendrils of flame. He saw some of the *Vimanas* exploding mid air, while some others dodged the eruptions from the earth. He saw many of these aerial machines circle smoldering land masses, and then head off into the horizon. He saw the smoldering land masses break into sections, many of which sank beneath the waves.

The three dimensional scenes then showed an armada of *Vimanas* soaring to a height that even the most hardy birds cannot soar, and then descending towards what looked like the contours of the Indian subcontinent. They explored the Himalayas and circled their great peaks, and studied the rivers that flowed down the mountains. Then they descended into North India, onto the banks of a river that was not far from the Himalayas. A thrill passed through Keith. He knew that the British Raj had initiated an archaeological survey in North India in the last century, and they had found the remnants of a mature civilization in this broad region, complete with sophisticated urban planning and indoor plumbing. He was probably seeing the forebears of that very civilization, laying down their roots.

The scenes shifted abruptly to another massive war, which included weapons of a destructive force that outmatched what he had seen in the battle scenes earlier. Explosive devices were employed by people who were perhaps descendants of the Atlanteans against one another, and thousands of people were erased in an instant. The numbers that died were beyond compare, and a river of fire rode through the air, melting and setting alight everything in its path. Smoke and ash billowed out for miles, and he saw people far away struck by maladies with their hair, skin and nails peeling off, and experiencing all manner of anguish.

Then the scenes changed, to show a cluster of *Vimanas* descending onto the jungle in the Congo, whose flora and fauna looked only too familiar. Then the magic show of light and sound vanished.

At the end of the week of quarantine, Jata and Gala came to speak with him.

"What you are about to see has only been seen by three people before you, in the history of your civilization," Gala said, giving him an unnervingly direct look. "We have been studying your biology for the last week, and we have concluded that you do not pose a threat to our colony. We also have concluded that we *may* pose a threat to you biologically. All three individuals who passed our tests did not survive exposure to our raw environment. We told them this, before allowing them into our world. Every one of them chose the same thing. To view the splendor of our civilization, knowing that they would be risking their lives.

Your biology appears largely similar to them. So, if you want to see us as we are, you will probably die within the week. You must choose what you want. You can have a life of quarantine, because we cannot allow you back into your world for many reasons. Or you can have knowledge, but the chances that you will die are high. Remember the stakes, and choose as you will."

Keith nodded. It was like Socrates and hemlock. Knowledge always extracted a price. The highest and most sacred knowledge was given to those individuals who chose to sacrifice their very existence on its altar. Perhaps this was the only way to learn everything that one cherished.

"Where do we start?" Keith said. "I have a lot to learn in a week."

May as well have an interesting time.

Author's Note

This is a work of fiction. There is no claim to historical or archaeological authenticity. It is meant to be long on imagination and makes no claims to being accurate on the facts.

CULTURE WAR

Jayant Avva

Things had to change! Sally saw that her cell culture had been contaminated. Growing a colony of Saccharomyces Cerevisiae (Baker's yeast) cells was usually much easier. But someone had contaminated her colony. She *knew* that it was deliberate sabotage, so she decided to find the culprit.

This wasn't the first time that this had happened. She had had a similar issue happen a couple of months earlier, and she had let it go. She had suspected that someone in her lab was trying to sabotage her work, and she suspected a number of individuals. When you work in a lab with more than twenty people, there tends to be some sense of herd protection. The culprit probably felt safe in the anonymity that being part of such a herd conveys.

She placed her cell culture in the regular fridge, *her* fridge, and went to find a spot in the lab where she could maintain a vigil for many hours at a stretch.

•

She awoke with a start. She was sitting next to one of the lab windows, which was situated in such a way that she would be mostly concealed from someone who entered the lab and approached her fridge. She watched. The form that appeared in the dim light appeared to be that of Virginie. That bitch! She had suspected that the Belgian graduate student was the one who was fucking her over.

140

She crept out of her hiding place, and then leapt into view, as she saw Virginie standing in her aisle.

"What are you doing here, Virginie?" she snarled.

The Belgian girl took a few moments to recover.

"Cheri, I must have walked into the wrong aisle," she said.

Sally wondered whether she should make a scene. There were no witnesses. What would be the result of the private tussle. What would calling her out in private, in the darkness of night, accomplish?

She watched as Virginie walked away.

•

"Motherf…!"

Sally didn't even have the energy to complete swearing. She had stayed all night in the lab, and had dozed off a couple of times, and then arose finally for getting some Starbucks before she came back to the lab. She had spent a total of an hour away.

The yeast cells were not as they should be. Contaminated with whatever devil's concoction the Belgian bitch had put in them. How could that be? Sally didn't know.

It was 8:30 am. She could hear her adviser speaking to someone. She decided to snoop around. She opened the door that led from the lab into the adviser's large ante-room, where they often had group meetings and did lots of thinking using a whiteboard and markers.

She heard Virginie's voice, and that maddening rolling R. Bitch!

Adrenaline flooded her system. She leapt into action. She picked up a molecular biology textbook and kicked open her adviser's ante-room door. Her adviser, Dr. Li, showed an expression of annoyance that quickly turned to concern and fear. Oh yeah, the Belgian bitch was having her PhD qualifier and the committee were prepping her. The smell of medium roast Pike was in the air. There were bagels, donuts, cream cheese and lox on one of the tables.

Sally barely registered the horror on the faces of the committee members, and Virginie's family members, and other assorted faces. She raised the book.

"You fucked with my yeast colony for the last time, bitch!"

Sally flung the textbook at Virginie. The spine of the book caught her on the jaw, and she staggered back against a wall. Dr. Li started yelling something about being suspended from the program, while also backing away from Sally. The heavyset Dr. Orozco, another of the committee members, tried to block Sally's progress, but then he stopped.

"Stop them Marc!" Dr. Li yelled at him.

"She is demonstrating the Sasquatch pose, I want to see this," Orozco said, reaching for a bagel.

"I agree with Marc, it is the Sasquatch pose," Dr. Alfonsi, the other committee member said. "I want to see it too."

She leaned back, and took another sip of her coffee.

Virginie stood poised on one leg, striking the famed Sasquatch pose. Sally struck the Shaolin Kung Fu's Twist stance. They circled each other, while the committee members backed away. Virginie's family yelled out their encouragement in the form of insults directed at Sally.

Virginie moved to strike Sally with all the finesse of a Shaolin monk. Her leg missed, as Sally expertly danced away, and then jabbed at her with her outstretched middle finger. Virginie moved into the finger, with her shoulder and broke it, and Sally screamed. She launched herself onto Virginie's back, and bit down on her shoulder.

Dr. Orozco spread lox on his bagel, contemplating the scene. Dr. Alfonsi sipped her coffee. Dr. Li saw both her students and her reputation slipping away. She didn't want to get into the melee. She pleaded with them to stop.

Virginie threw Sally over her head, so that Sally landed on the food table. Dr. Orozco smiled, seeing as how he'd gotten the last bagel before everything landed on the floor. The table broke, and a dazed Sally staggered to her feet. Adrenaline was keeping her going.

Virginie struck the Sasquatch pose once again. Sally struck the crane pose. They leaped at each other. Molecular biology could wait for another day.

Author's Note

This story doesn't take itself seriously. I hope it makes you laugh. I was trying to come up with a fairly ridiculous way to spin an academic rivalry, and I decided on a martial arts fight in a conference room. In case you were wondering, I made up the Sasquatch pose, because - why not?

HVAC

Mitchell Harris

It was on the 27th day since I'd left my apartment that the knock on the door came. When I opened it door and before me stood a big man in overalls, with a bowl haircut and an enormous nose, too large for his face. He snorted a long snort and I heard the snot in it.

"HVAC," he said. He carried a bright red toolbox.

"I'm sorry?" I replied, still holding the door open, its smooth wood in my hand.

"'m here about the heater. Didincha get the notice yesterday? 24 hrs notice to enter, 'tis the law, ya know."

I tried to remember. Did I get a notice yesterday? Was that the piece of paper I'd thrown away without a second thought, or had that been a piece of unopened mail?

"Oh, yeah, sure. Come on in. Do what you have to do."

"Thanks," he said. "Shouldn't take long."

I let the stranger into my apartment. I sat back down on the couch and kept watching Archie Bunker complain about this and that. The audience laughed uproariously. The HVAC man walked into the corner of the room, next to the vent set into the wall and the tall metal of the unit beneath it and put his toolbox down. I saw his hairy arm, and a scabby patch of flesh just by his elbow, bright red. He coughed, a disgusting sound, full of phlegm, and pulled a rag from the front pocket of his overalls. He coughed and coughed again into the rag, holding it over his mouth.

"Sorry," he said. "Bad cold." He snorted again.

He rustled around in his toolbox noisily. It made it hard for me to focus on the show. I wished he wasn't there. He pulled things from his toolbox, I saw: a screwdriver, a wrench, something that looked like a multimeter. And a glass tube. I watched him raise it above his face and peer into its depths. He pulled a cork from the end and held it near the vent. I thought this very odd.

"What are you doing?" I said. Archie was still arguing. I wondered if he was really very upset and no one cared. If he was sad inside. The audience just kept laughing.

"Hrm?" he snorted again. "Oh, air quality test. Standard procedure."

I said nothing and kept watching the show. The HVAC man rustled around in his toolbox some more. Out of the corner of my eye I saw him remove the vent cover and rummage around inside. I saw him replace it. The credits rolled and the music played.

"All done," he said, and coughed once more, this time into this hand.

"Great," I said, making no effort to hide my disgust.

"Best be going," he replied, gathering up his things. "Have a great night then!"

"Yes, you too," I said, inwardly annoyed. I watched him leave and heard the door slam closed behind him and our time together.

It was dark in the apartment save for the light of the TV. The next episode started. Halfway through, the heater clicked on and hummed.

•

When I woke up, I was on the couch and my chest hurt. I coughed, and I could feel the bones of my ribs. The TV was still blaring. I walked over to the bedroom and crawled back into my safe haven and the sheets and comforter were warm and heavy. I just wanted to lie beneath them and never come out again. I just wanted the outside world to go away.

I woke up later, the afternoon sun pouring in through the blinds. I watched motes of dust dance their illuminated dance in rays of light splitting the dry air of the room.

I walked to the bathroom and looked at myself in the mirror. My skin was pale and beneath my eyes dark circles. It seemed to me like they had been there forever. I pulled down the skin under my left eye and looked into the white of my sclera. It was more a pinkish-white, split with tiny arcing red lines of angry blood vessels.

Why, they screamed back at me from the mirror. *Why are you doing this to us? Why won't you get up? Why won't you just leave your apartment?*

Pain gripped my chest again and I could feel the bones of my ribs in chest once more. I hacked a hacking cough and hot irons stabbed me. Something was not right. I fell from my feet down next to the toilet and its white porcelain laid expectantly before me.

Oh, it's you, I heard it say. *So funny to see you this way, who's the big man now, King of the Castle? I know your secrets. I know the things that come out of your body. I know the long days and long nights you've sat here in the darkn, trying to push the sadness away with all the drink, only to throw it all up to me after. I know you. You can't hide from me.*

"Fuck you," I said aloud. I vomited. My guts wrenched and I heaved dry heaves. In the clear water of the bowl ejecta was green and solid. Looking at it made my insides tighten again and I could feel the stabbing pain of the hot pitchforks in my sides.

We're all in this together. Me and your eyes. Your bed. The TV, silently judging you. Maybe if you'd clean me more often, I wouldn't treat you this way, the white porcelain thought back at me. *Maybe then I wouldn't side with your bed. And your sclera. You're so pathetic, you sad little man. I hope you die and they find you with your face down in my tepid water and your own puke.*

Everything was becoming hazy. The room was spinning and the tile of the bathroom walls was white, so white like the porcelain before me but now it was deforming and twisting and shifting and all I could here was the screaming of the commode before me and my sclera within my head and my bed, far away in the bedroom beneath the rumpled sheets I'd thrown off of me and the comforter I'd kicked into the corner and they were all screaming: *You worthless piece of shit. You worm. Get out. Go out. Make something of yourself. Or just fucking DIE already. Just stay here with your drink and your comic books and your Archie Bunker and just fucking DIE.*

And I held my hands against my ears and I moaned but still it wasn't enough to stop their cries, to stop the torment, and deep down, really deep down, I knew they were right and it hurt worse than any pain my ribs could ever feel. I saw my uncle looking across the room at me at convocation and the eyes upon me and the thoughts of everyone in the room as I walked across the stage, and I knew, I just knew, that none of their thoughts were about me, no one cared about *me,* all they saw when they saw me was my dead father and the thought of him and the car swerving and flipping and rolling down the cold hard wet pavement of the highway that night and twisting into a tangled mess of metal against that lamppost, and The Dean shook my hand and handed me my diploma and I felt the bright lights of the stage above us shine down on illuminating me for all to see and I could hear the thoughts of the audience bursting forth from their minds into the air around them and all they said was *what a waste, what a waste, who will take up the torch now? Is this pathetic boy of a man going to be the one to take over such an empire? No, no, no... tut tut tut.*

I wretched again, a dry heave. There was nothing left. *You're pathetic,* I heard within me. It was my pupils now. My sclera had been talking with them and convinced them to rise up against me. *I hope you die and no one finds you this way. I hope you rot to death with your head in this toilet bowl.*

The toilet laughed.

•

When I woke up, I was in my bed again. My ribs felt like they been pulled out of my flesh and pushed back in. Like Mohammed Ali had done 100 rounds on me. Mike Tyson had used them as his speed bag then spat in my face and laughed. "Them's the breaks, champ," I saw him lisp. His face tattoo moved strangely when talked. "Nothing personal. Hope everything turns out for you."

I threw on my Black Sabbath t-shirt from the floor; I thought it smelled funny and some stain, something oily, had ruined the front of it; when had that happened? Jeans too, followed. I needed to get out here. Something had changed. The air was different somehow. It felt hot. Everything felt like it was collapsing around me and enveloping me in a sticky claustrophobia. And I could feel the toilet waiting for me quietly in the bathroom, smirking to itself and plotting against me.

Click, click, the locked turned and I stepped out into the hall. The old fluorescent lights flickered above and the one three down was still burnt out. Shadows were long against the dirty carpeting of the hallway.

I walked to the elevator and pushed the button for 'G', the one that never lit up. The tiny elevator lurched and then decided to make its way down. It was grimy and smelled like ass. The mirrors on either side reflected me in a never-ending pattern, thousands of copies of me, millions, repeating forever into nothingness. I wondered if any of them ever went outside. If any of them weren't a failure.

Finally the elevator lurched again as it reached the ground the floor. There was no ding but the doors opened and made a sound. Before me, the lobby. I hated the lobby because I knew that at the end of the lobby was the tall floor-to-ceiling glass windows and beyond those windows was *the outside world* and that was a world I didn't want to step back into. No matter how dark it was in my apartment. No matter how cruel my toilet, my bed, and the whites and pupils of my eyes might be to me; because whatever was inside was safe and known and understood but the things and people out there were not. Sometimes when I came down I saw people come in from the cruel, cold, dark world out there and they looked different than me: they wore long coats and fancy clothes and their hair was beautiful and long and fell to their shoulders and I wondered what it must be like to be so beautiful, so wanted, so successful. But whenever I thought about these things all I could think about was my uncle and the burning wreck of my father's Mercedes and how black his casket had been.

The concierge stood behind the counter, behind his wall of refuge, looking down at mounds of papers and undelivered packages, at computer mice and a heavy black Maglite and keys to the security room and a weird round one for the elevator and I wondered if he was happy or if he ever got lonely like me. I saw him touch the flashlight and I wondered whether he'd ever even had to use it.

There was a sound and the doors opened and out of them walked a beautiful Asian man and at his side was an even more beautiful Asian woman, with long flowing black hair. The man wore a tan trenchcoat with the belt undone and falling at his sides, just so.

"Good evening, Maurice," he said. And I saw that his teeth were straight and clean and beautiful and impossibly white, like lines of chiclets, and the concierge said back to him *Good Evening Sir.*

I coughed loudly and the sound shattered the perfectness of the lobby. The concierge and the beautiful Asian couple both stared at me in my ratty t-shirt and jeans and I coughed again and this time I felt phlegm in my throat and it made the disgusting phlegmy sound, just like the HVAC man when he'd come up to my apartment.

The man made a face, scowled and the girl pulled closer to him and whispered something into his ear. They disappeared toward the elevator banks.

"Can I..." - the concierge was hesitant in his manner - "help you?"

"Hi, yes, I," My throat felt scratchy and strange, and I just noticed it was hot down here too, too hot and the air was stifling. Was there something wrong with the whole building? "Yes, I think, there's, there is... there's something..."

The concierge kept his hands down on the counter before him. He didn't look at me, then slowly looked up at me and into my eyes. I saw in his face what I'd felt before when the stranger, the HVAC man, had come into my apartment unannounced and unwelcome: *disgust.*

"I think there's something wrong with my apartment," I finally said. "It's... it's... too hot. The air, there's something wrong with the air."

The concierge stared at me.

"The HVAC man," I said. My words were coming out all funny. Something was wrong. Why didn't he understand me? Why was he looking at me like that? "The man who came yesterday" - *it was yesterday, wasn't it?* - "to fix the heater? I think something is not quite right because now it's *hot,* so *hot,* too HOT in my apartment and I don't know what to do."

"Someone came to look at your heater?" The concierge said. He brushed a strand of his hair away from his face. He paused. "Yesterday?"

"Yes, he said, he left a notice... 24 hrs notice" - *'tis the law, he'd said* - "for entry. Are they fixing checking all the units? I think he didn't check mine correctly. I think there may be something *wrong.* I think he may have done something *wrong.*" And the word *wrong* was like a hot glob of metal, like a jagged piece of metal sticking out of my face, burning and piercing and revealing me for the fraud I was. And in my mind I heard the voice of the toilet again *oh God no, not you again, please stop* only now the voice wasn't it anymore, it was the voice of my Uncle and I saw his piercing blue eyes staring across the gymnasium and piercing into me, right through me and it *hurt* oh God, it *hurt* and I just heard him say with those eyes *won't you listen to your self, you little piece of shit? He doesn't know what the hell you're talking about and he thinks you're crazy and you've a failure and you've always been a failure and nothing you will ever do will change that.*

The concierge paused. He looked at me with a seriousness in his eyes. He paused and then he spoke.

"We haven't been running any checks on the units," he said. "We won't be doing that for another few weeks until when we switch off the heat for the summer. And when we are that sort of thing should be done by the super."

I felt sick. The wrongness had somehow seeped out of the air and away from the idea of the HVAC man and his wrench and his red toolbox and multimeter and glass tube and into my mouth and then inside of me into my lungs. The room was spinning.

"It's hot, so hot," I said aloud. I saw the pearly whites of the beautiful Asian man and then my Uncle's stark blue eyes.

"Sir, are you alright?" the concierge said. He was staring at me and I realized I'd not spoken aloud at all.

"Yes, I'm" - the painting. The painting behind the desk. Had it always been there? Or wait, yes it had, but it had it always been that colour? It seemed... greener now. No, no, it had always been green but now it was a deeper shade of green. I stared into the depths of it and the long stalks of grass they looked real, as if they were really waving in the wind, blowing in the breeze over the dark soil of the farmland's earth, and I heard the wind whistling and then far off a dog barking and the sound of a lawn mower, and of a pickup truck backfiring and then bales of straw being stabbed on pitchforks and throw in big piles in the rafters of the hayloft and I smelled the stale yellow smell of the dried grass and from it came

"Sir?" The concierge was still staring. The painting behind him was just stripes of green paint on black.

"Yes, I'm," *fine. The word you're looking for is fine.* "I'm..." *say it. say it. say 'fine'.*

"I'm..." And then I exploded into coughing, spasms wracking my body and the coughs burned and hurt until finally they subsided and I stood, hunched over, in front of the counter gasping for breath. "fine."

I walked back toward the elevator bank, following the path of the beautiful Asian man, and I heard the lights buzzing. I pushed the button and it lit up and the elevator came down to G and the doors opened and there was no ding.

•

"The President has made it clear that his stance on negotiating with terrorists will not change, however, pundits in Washington are saying that there is doubt amongst his inner circles and calls for an exception to be made in this highly unprecedented case..."

On the TV, strong winds blew and I watched the anchor struggle to fight them. I heard the sound of the air buffeting her mic. She pulled her coat closer around her and it flapped.

"...the real question, in this difficult time, is what the expected outcome is, and what the correct response should be, given the ambiguity of the demands presented forth, and whether the communication can be trusted given that it only appeared on social media, from an unverified Twitter account..."

I pushed the button on the remote and the reporter and the howling wind around her disappeared into a wink of light in the center of the black screen. And then, there I sat, as I had for so many hours before, in the blackness of my empty apartment. The silence judged me, until the heater clicked on again, and I heard the air rushing from between the slats of the grate, out into the room around.

The sound of the air rushing was quiet, a dull droning that faded into the background, the sort of thing you wouldn't even notice. But I noticed. And as I slowly walked toward the grate in the wall and the metal beneath it, I felt in my chest a cold hand grabbing hold of my beating heart and that hand was squeezing and it and it was racing and all around it was just ribs, ribs, ribs ready to be yanked from my bloody flesh and stabbed back into me.

And I walked over toward the vent and I saw that the screws in the wall weren't screwed in and the grate was just sitting there in place and then I saw my hands reach up and grab it and my fingernails dig beneath and pull and I heard the sound of the grate coming away from the wall and it sounded metal and plaster and air.

The air it kept droning and now it was a warm wave against my face and in the air I could see tiny white particles, tiny white balls of dust and out into the room they escaped until they faded away and appeared invisible. And standing up on my tip-toes looking into the vent, I saw what was hidden in the vent, tucked back into the depths of its throat - tiny black globes, in a bunch like grapes - and I saw the globes were pulsating, growing larger and smaller, like breaths, like the pulses of my strangled beating heart, and on the globes there were veins crawling and when the globes pulsed I saw the white motes escaped from them and out into the air of the vent and then my living room and I saw my Father's dead dry cracked lips move and heard the word in my mind as clear as if he'd whispered it in my ear: *spores*.

And then those dry cracked lips were those of the HVAC man and now they were moving impossibly fast, faster than human lips could ever move, forming no words, but still I heard the words - I heard *the idea* of the words in my mind, over and over:

air quality test, standard procedure

Air Quality Test, standard procedure

AiR QualitY teSt, StandArD PROCEdure

AIR quality TEST

Air qUalItY tEsT

AIR QUALITY test

AIR QUALITY TEST

AIR QUALITY TEST

TeSt

tEsT

tEST

tEST

tEST

and it was the tube. The tube. The tube he opened. That's what it was.

I put the vent cover back in place. Outside my window, the sun was setting. I looked down at my arm beneath the black sleeve of my Black Sabbath t-shirt, and on it I saw the same scabby patch of flesh next to my elbow that HVAC man had. It itched terribly and I scratched it. I thought for a second about the lobby and the concierge and the beautiful Asian couple with the beautiful man and his beautiful chiclet teeth and they weren't judging me now, no they weren't judging me now, they were my friends and I could be their friend and I should have just gone and tried to help them.

And for once I had the strangest feeling: *I wanted to go outside.* I wanted to see other people and let them know how I felt.

I walked out toward the door I felt the sheets of the bedroom smiling at me and the toilet was happy now he was grinning at me with his beautiful porcelain mouth and my eyes were happy in my head and the veins, I couldn't see them but I knew they'd faded away, the angry red lines, the bloodshot vessels begging me to *just get out.*

The elevator dinged when it reached the ground floor this time. I walked out toward the concierge and behind him I saw the waving green grasses of the fields. And from the tops of the waving green grasses the waving green grasses were going to seed and the seeds were blowing in the wind, out over the fields of farmland, and I smiled because there was something familiar about that, something I recognized and it made me feel happy.

"Everything ok, sir?" The concierge said. Rays of the sunset were pouring in through the windows above us, into the air of the lobby and onto the hard tiles of the floor.

"Yes, yes," I said, smiling. "Everything's fine." And when I spoke the last word I walked by the counter before the man, by the wall guarding his little safe haven, and I exhaled. I watched the white motes in my breath danced in the illuminated air between us like dandelion seeds and I saw him breathe them in.

I smiled and walked away and out toward the door, to the outside world. It was a beautiful evening.

It had been far too long since I'd been outside.

Author's Note

Writing this was an interesting exercise for me, as there was a point where the story sort of took on a life of its own - the finished work ending up much more avant-garde and surreal than expected. My initial idea was for a straightforward body horror story, 'colony' referring to the spores infecting human bodies and causing their hosts to continue spreading them. I think the final story plays on themes other than just that of (bodily) disease: mental illness, isolation, our modern urban 'colonies' of strangers living together, and how much we really know about and can trust those around us.

THE BREATH

Emil Pellim

The stick connects with the rock for the last time of the day. This final clank is the only which pleases Dessa's ears instead of boring into them.

The baritone whispers of the ocean cleanse the aural holes on her walk home, like a cool disinfectant. They are the last sounds of any significance that Dessa will hear today; she casts them aside with the closing door as she enters her lonesome abode. Never married, her home houses silence, not spouse. She places her banging stick in the corner closest to the door, where it too can rest in silence for a few hours.

As usual, Dessa finds the log-carved table in the main room to be covered with fresh fruit, most of which could have never grown in the climate of their town. Next to them are several pouches of nuts and legumes: the contents glisten in the lamplight. A crudely woven white fabric plays placemat for a loaf of rye bread with perfect crust. The smell suggests it to have just finished baking, and could make a person full feel famished. The walls look freshly spackled too - the crack in the dividing one between main room and bedroom has been repaired. As gods, the Shefove are as generous as they were demanding, and they are clearly pleased with her noisemaking today.

Before tasting any of the food herself, Dessa brings her raggedy carrying sack out of the bedroom, and sets it on one of the crooked wood-carved chairs next to the table. She uses a knife to cut the loaf in uneven halves, and places the much-bigger at the bottom of the sack where it would hopefully be confined enough to not dry out before tomorrow's eve. A small handful of nuts from each pouch is relocated to a bowl, and the remainder, almost all, are added to the sack. They hold well in time and she prefers to add a greater fraction of the nuts than fruit, which rot quite quickly. Nevertheless, she tops off the care package with several of each type of fruit, and ties the top of the bag.

With that done, she sits on the same chair that had held the sack, and samples all the foods in order. Dessa's mind empties of all other thought as she indulges in one of the few pleasures left in her life - she focuses on the fibre strings of the ripe mangos dissolving on her tongue, on the small seeds of the wild strawberries scraping her throat lightly as she swallows, on the explosions of oversweet juices as she bites into bright green grapes. Some food remains, and Dessa wraps it up in the woven cloth after shaking it loose of breadcrumbs. She adds it to the sack prepared earlier.

The evening typically offers Dessa some hours for reading handwritten creations of the people at the Breath. One of the neighbors had made last month's delivery, now known to be penultimate, and her nephew Darba sent her a giant bundle of writings back with him. When the people at the Breath wrote, they kept little. They were media, transmitters; once they consumed Bedna's Breath, they produced it right out. In the past, people like Dessa would be entitled to a smaller fraction of the output - but interest in it decreased with time. Her passion is rare to be seen now, and she receives more than enough to fill every bit of her spare time.

This night, she does no reading. The next day will be arduous for Dessa. Hours of worship to start, followed by a trek to the Breath and back to make the delivery. Worst of all, she'll have to deliver the announcement too. The old woman thinks it better to quiet her brain with sleep than stay up. She brings some lumber from outside the house and puts it in the firepit, filling both the main room and the bedroom with heat and swarms of smoke. Dessa disrobes and throws her clothes onto the back of the chair in a messy pile, then slips under the heavy wool blanket sprawled on her bed.

The moon and stars announce the night, then float along with it leisurely. Dessa's chest rides shallow breaths in her anxious sleep. Around her, the room begins to deteriorate. Chips flake and float off of the wall opposite her bed like dandruff. The metal-cast cups in the kitchen develop rust stains. The washing basin droops like wax and leaks moisture onto the floor. The only object in the home unaffected by the rapid decay is a carved wooden statue on a small shelf in the bedroom. It is yet another form of Bedna's Breath - Darba had inhaled that particular one and exhaled it in the form of this statue, later gifting it to his dear aunt. It is an anchor in a sea of dissolving material. She looks to it for a dose of beauty and happiness when needed, to override the daily desolation of her decaying world.

Dessa awakes to the increased disarray and blinks tired lids. The sun shines through a window and its heavy rays fall on her breasts. The new day's light feels oppressive as it normally does, just a signal for the start of a pre-decided routine of worship. On her way out, she ties the end of the full sack around her banging stick, and then props it up on her shoulder for her walk to worship, as she'll be headed to town square straight from there. The closing door behind her makes a creak it hadn't last time it was opened.

She heaves under the sack's weight all the way, swallowing the salty mist of the ocean with laboured inhales. The path Dessa takes intersects many other townspeople who were either much swifter to rise, or had chosen to worship in the late night and early morning. A man half-buries a stone into the wet sand at the edge of the water, waits for a half dozen waves to wash the muddy hut off of it, then starts the process over again. Dessa waves but he waves her off with a sand-covered paw. Further down the shore, a woman plucks small fish out of the water with her bare hands. Every time she catches one, she extends her fish-containing closed fist straight out, rotates about herself in a circle, and then opens her palm to plop the fish back into the water. She gives a warmer greeting as Dessa passes, and a "see you tonight."

Once at her rock, Dessa sets the sack down and unties it from her instrument. She takes a deep breath to clear her mind of everything, of expectation, and raises the stick in the air high above her head. It comes down and connects with the rock, sending a dull clank through the air. Not so unpleasant on its own, but ever more so as part of a set with all the upcoming ones. Dessa raises the stick, and strikes again. Raises and strikes. Stick up and strikes again. Clank. Again the stick goes up. Clank. Clank. There's a rhythm to it. It's not a rhythm of human life. It's that of the Shefove gods. Another hit with the stick, another. Raising it and lowering her arm with power. Clank. She hates the song she plays, a god's treasure but a human's tripe. She hits for many hours. They will be happy, the fruit will be ample.

When done, Dessa carries the sack of consumables to the town square. The townsworkers have loaded the cart already and the horses are being fed to give them energy for the trip to the Breath of Bedna, three hours trot each way. The provisions from the town fill half of the cart. Dessa throws her own sack into the official pile, and others do so too. Some are family members of people living at the Breath. Some simply admirers of Bedna's speech in all its forms. Tension and tears appear on most faces - they see that the gifts are many but pale in size to the town's own contribution. The fishcatching woman throws a final bag on top and nods to Dessa with wet eyes during departure.

The animals run tirelessly under Dessa's direction for hours. The Breath of Bedna has no clear outer boundary, some can sense it further than others due to their own perceptions. A distant song slowly becomes audible over the gallops of the horses, Dessa ascertains it as real after a few dismissals of it as an apparition of sound. She slows the horses and she can hear more clear. The tone, the rasp, are unmistakable. The fishcatcher's daughter Pesen sits on a large rock and transforms the Breath into a melancholic melody that meanders between notes, between sorrow and quiet content, too. The two of them unload the mother's bag and the song stops for a moment while Pesen swallows the flesh of fruit hungrily. The same song sends off Dessa deeper.

She passes others with no personal presents, no parents or others to send them. They'll be the most affected by the decision, and Dessa requests they follow to the core of the Breath. They walk behind, eyeing dried meats protruding from woven bags on the back of the cart. They reach the centre, which looks like a museum of Bedna's soul. Her Breath is visible all around, in charcoal drawings on rocks, in carvings of statuettes, even in the pruning of plants into shapes that express Her deepest emotions.

Darba is there; he is in the process of Breathing. He sprays paint made of crushed bugs and beetroot skins onto a rock canvas, conjuring a stunning spectacle of colour. Dessa and the followers let him finish as they unload the cart of provisions. After his trance concludes, Darba rejects the bag of gifts from his aunt and throws it onto the official communal pile sent from the town to be shared with everyone. He does so with every transfer of Shefove worship spoils that he receives from Dessa.

Hungry men and women of all ages sit and eat with dirty hands, grabbing from bags and chewing slowly to savour each bite. They urge Dessa to eat but she pretends. She's starved from the trip, but she refuses to take a single bite of this already too little allotment. Let her body feast on its own fat - she'll worship herself more food tomorrow.

For a bitter dessert, Dessa serves the decision of the town's tribunal. The Shefove worshippers will no longer be sending official shipments of food to the Breathers. The majority of them don't have family here, nor consume much of the output, and thus do not wish to give up their own Shefove gifts. Dessa speaks with shame as if decisionmaker and not just messenger, apologizing constantly. The mounds of bags lie to the side as a reminder that those sent by family cannot compare in number to those donated by the town - the former all the future holds.

This time the cart carries no output from the Breath on the return trip. The horses struggle under the weight of a dozen people who have chosen to move back to town and worship. Most are those with children. They pass by Pesen on the way out who is still Breathing, singing. One of the lucky ones, whose mother sends plenty. Her song has changed into a more upbeat tune, with a naive hope icing over darker currents. Dessa stops as to quiet the animals, and closes her eyes. She inscribes the song in her memory note by note. During worship tomorrow, she will rewrite every ugly clank of the stick with it.

Author's Note

This was supposed to be 2000 words more detailed with a lot more description... but I spent those words on Scruff as a distraction while writing at the bar instead.

CŌLONY

David F. Shultz

A government agent walked into a bar.

And in an alien world, a technician named Klef trembled along with the pink walls of his podcraft. Far ahead, the enormous orb of the "Blue Galaxy" expanded before the intergalactic pioneers. Though their fleet measured in the millions, colony ships and battlecruisers and podcrafts, they were miniscule in comparison to this goliath expanse of unexplored worlds, which could provide home to trillions-and-trillions of future generations of Klef's people — or perhaps swallow and destroy them all, before they even settled.

Lord Commander's voice rang out inside Klef's pod. Klef could not focus on the words, distracted by the encompassing sheen of the Blue Galaxy, which had overtaken his monitor. He was aware of only Lord Commander's intonation. The speech was meant as a stirring oratory — to inspire courage among the millions of pioneers into this unknown expanse. Klef picked up the odd words here or there, like "new home" and "future" and "our people", but those things all disappeared into the watery depths of the Blue Galaxy on Klef's viewscreen. Klef was not cut out for exploration. He nearly glebbed his yarks.

The fleet breached the outer shell of the Blue Galaxy, and alarms blared. The formation was breaking up, struggling against the onslaught of particles that swirled in the outer edges of the Blue Galaxy, increasing in density as they descended further towards their destination — the solid, galactic core.

"Hold formation," Lord Commander's voice demanded. The coordinates and trajectory correctives flashed on Klef's screen. There was their destination, thousands-upon-thousands of blorzons in the distance towards the galactic core, so mind-bogglingly massive that it defied all physical explanation. And yet there it was, confirmed by the scanners. And on the surface of the galactic core, at their landing site: thousands of red worlds, perhaps everything their people would need to ensure their survival, if only they could reach them.

Klef watched over the hours with sadness and increasing trepidation as lights blinked away from the surviving fleet manifest, poddies blown off-course by galactic currents, swept alone into the unfathomable abyss — lost forever in this alien galaxy.

Klaxons screamed, and Lord Commander spoke.

"Approaching a barrier of unknown material. Perhaps a force field. Brace for impact, and prepare for casualties."

Klef watched the viewscreen with horror. On the fleet manifest, thousands of lights blinked out in rapid succession, battlecruisers annihilated, whole colony ships, too. Millions of people, wiped out against the surface of this alien world. He approached the barrier, or the forcefield, or whatever it was. Three. Two. One.

Klef awoke, his body stiff and sore, his skin burning everywhere. The ground was red, endless fields of red, except where it was punctured by smoking wreckage of the fleet. Shards of podships here and there. And just towards the horizon, the shattered and strewn debris of the fleet's flagship, the Nova Sentinel. Their command vessel. And the best among them. The wise and strong and honourable. All lost.

Klef struggled to his feet and stumbled to the wreckage. Had their journey all been for naught? Was this how they would meet their end? Klef stumbled, dragging his broken leg across the alien terrain. At least he could be breathe, and move, but without the resources of the fleet, survival was impossible.

Figures moved in the distance, near the wreckage of the Nova Sentinel. Klef hurried his pace, grimacing against the pain, and the figures came more clearly into view. Soldiers and medics rushing about, attending to victims of the crash. Survivors! Superior officers shouted over the chaos, trying to maintain order among panicking pioneers. And bodies, bodies everywhere — and pieces of them.

An orderly pack of armed men approached Klef from the distance, with high-ranking insignia and imposing energy rifles. Why had they singled him out? And who was the figure in the center of their protective formation? Klef headed to meet them.

"Are you a pod technician?" said one of the soldiers.

Klef nodded. They must have recognized his insignia, or else scanned his pod beacon for technical assets.

The men opened their formation, and revealed the figure behind the wall of their bodies. The high spiked shoulders of his black uniform, the shimmering pendant, and his command regalia — Lord Commander. Klef dropped to his knees, and one of the soldiers gave the introductory address on the Lord Commander's behalf.

"Galactic Regent and Prefect of the Apical Honour Guard, Lord Commander Parmplesnärfs," the soldier said, and added, "You, pod technician, you may stand state your name."

"I am Klef," he said.

"Klef, pod technician," the Lord Commander said. "Our own pod technicians aboard the Nova Sentinel did not survive the crash. You will join us. Together, we will establish our new colony."

Klef looked with new eyes at the red world around him. Strewn with dead bodies and smouldering wreckage. And yet, milling around all this destruction, were workers and soldiers and medics and leaders. Capable, strong, and willing. And Lord Commander had survived. There was hope. Klef would do his part, and perhaps this place would come to be their home, and not their doom.

Back on Earth, in Windsor, Ontario, CSIS special agent Adam Hedman knocked on a door.

A strong-looking woman in overalls opened the door. "Yes?"

"Are you Linda White?"

"I'm Linda, yeah. How can I help you, mister..."

"Special Agent Hedman," he said, extending a hand. "I work for CSIS. An investigator. Oh don't worry! You're in no trouble at all — I was just hoping to ask you some questions, for the safety of your community."

"Is this about terrorism?" Linda said, failing to notice, or ignoring, Adam's extended hand. "Didn't think we'd get terrorists all the way out here."

"I'm not at liberty to say," Adam said, his hand still dangling awkwardly in the air,"though it is in the best interests of national security, and I would really appreciate your help. It will only take a minute."

Linda eyed him skeptically, his badge, and his extended hand, which she eventually shook.

She smiled politely. "How can I help you?"

"There was some unusual activity reported in the area," Adam said, careful to speak in appropriately vague terms. He chose not to reveal the leading theory, that it was a Russian spy satellite that had broken up on entry, depositing debris over a small area of Windsor,

Ontario. Linda White's property happened to be near the center of the radius. "Did you see or hear anything unusual last Friday, around three AM?"

"I was asleep," Linda said. "But, come to think of it, I did notice something unusual. In fact, I can show you!"

"Please."

Linda led Adam around the back of her house, to a large plot with several greenhouses. She grew tomatoes. It was neatly arranged within the greenhouse, a professional layout for a large tomato growing operation.

"Canadians eat more ketchup than anyone else on Earth!" Linda said, touring Adam through the rows of tomatoes. "We love our ketchup. Some people call it catsup. Ha! Did you know ketchup chips are Canadian only? Don't have those in the US-of-A. Well, Canadians love their tomatoes, and someone's got to grow 'em! That's where the real value is. Tomatoes! Anyways, there's what I wanted to show you. Up there."

"What am I looking for?"

"Those cracks. They weren't there before Friday."

Tiny cracks were on the glass, barely visible, hardly more than a spider web.

"There's more," Linda said. "Over there. And there."

"I see. I mean, almost. They're pretty small. They almost look like scratches. You're sure those weren't there before?"

"Oh, I'm sure. I'm in here every day. You think it could have something to do with those terrorists?"

"No," Adam said. "Certainly not. I wouldn't worry about that." Despite Linda's fears, terrorists had, in all probability, not come to Windsor to make small cracks in her greenhouse. But, microscopic debris from a Russian spy satellite could very well be the culprit.

"Oh, thank goodness!"

Adam's stomach grumbled, quite audibly.

"Oh dear. Hungry are you? Working hard today?"

"I've been interviewing all day."

"Then you need a break! Come on, agent Hedman — or do you prefer Adam? How about something to eat?"

"Adam is fine. And I really shouldn't."

"It's the least I could do! You're helping keep us safe. Thank goodness for you. I'd like to say thanks somehow!"

"I can't really spare the time."

"Oh, it'll just take a few minutes. And how will you work on an empty stomach? It'll just distract you all day. You need to eat!"

Linda was insistent. Adam consented. He was soon sitting at a comfortable wooden table in Linda's kitchen. Linda offered a beer, and Adam accepted a glass of water. Then she set down a plate with a burrito.

"My speciality," Linda said. "Best in the city, people say! It's the fresh tomatoes!"

Adam ate, and his mind wandered. He thought about the Russian spy-satellite, or whatever it was. Part of him expected it was something more mundane, like a college kid doing experiments with a drone, and part of him hoped it was something more fanciful and unexpected — maybe aliens. While he ate, in the height of his fancy, the burrito was an organic, tubular spaceship, and he was a gigantic, devouring beast. And, for the briefest Freudian moment, he focussed on the girth of the burrito and the surplus of sauce.

Adam thanked Linda for the burrito and her hospitality. Then he planned to put in a requisition to investigate the area. The cracks in the greenhouse glass suggested, perhaps, that something was amiss. Adam was determined to be the agent who would get to the bottom of it.

And, perhaps less than an hour prior, in a world that Adam could not possibly comprehend, an alien named Klef surveyed the progress of his colony, under the probing eye of Lord Commander Parmplesnärfs.

"We have functioning refineries and gestational pods," Klef said. "And fully operational seed blankets, at twelve gorbos."

"Is this sufficient?"

"It is sustainable," Klef said. "Without additional resources, we can't expand population at greater than point-two-percent. But, barring catastrophe, the colony can be sustained."

Lord Commander nodded, and turned his imposing figure towards the captain of operational command. "Prepare a scouting mission for the red planet's surface."

"Thy will be done," the captain said. He bowed, about-faced, and marched to the command growth.

The sky darkened. Buildings shook free from their foundations. The surface was a sudden flurry of chaos, soldiers leaping to the defense of Parmplesnärfs, and Klef felt himself lifted by pairs of hands, and shielded by bodies. He was carried by stronger people to the shelter.

The world rumbled.

"Are we under attack?" Lord Commander said.

"It appears to be a gravitational anomaly," an analyst said.

Indeed, as Klef surveyed the sensor readout data, it appeared the planet had shaken free of that great, green galactic mass that had kept it tethered in space. It was moving now, shooting through the galaxy at impossible speeds, in something resembling a sin-wave.

"Casualties?"

"Reports still coming in."

"Orders, sir?"

"Grow a defensive matrix," Lord Commander ordered.

This was Klef's job, as pod technician. He leapt from the seat where he had been deposited, towards the pod controls. He calibrated the genetic constraints, diverted seed energy, and invested growth resources in a general defense matrix. With no idea what was coming, there was no way to efficiently allocate energy, but, for the same reason, it was a necessary action. They had no idea what was coming.

"Defensive matrix gestating," Klef said. And soon, the colony walls had developed a thick, protective chamber against whatever was coming.

The shelter shook with enough force to throw Klef from his chair. He stood, and saw the others all doing likewise, grabbing on to handholds. Cracks formed in the walls, only slowly healed by their dwindling seed energy.

"Oh! My! Slurns!" the analyst said, and stared at the readout.

"What is it?" Lord Commander said.

"It's the planet. It's breaking up!"

Klef watched the scanner readouts of the planet. The once-perfect orb of red was sheared in slices. The slices in turn were sheared again, perpendicular to the first lines. Another set of shearing lines appeared, tearing the remaining strips of the planet into cubes.

"Will the colony be hit?" Lord Commander said.

Klef looked at the monitor, and the approaching lines of planet-destroying force. They would be.

With a world-shattering blast, the lights went out.

Emergency lights blinked back on.

"Casualty report," Lord Commander said.

"We've lost two-thirds of the colony, sir."

There was no time to mourn the dead. The next wave came suddenly.

"What in Slurn's name?" someone shouted from the darkness.

What was left of the planet, and the colony, was blasted with a super-heated wave of dihydrogen monoxide, so much thermal energy it blocked their scanners. The whole universe outside of the colony was, as far as they could tell, nothing more than boiling heat.

"Will the defensive matrix hold?"

Klef checked the readout. It was possible. But not without draining most of their precious reserves of seed energy.

"It might," Klef said. "But the growth reserves—"

"Put ninety-percent of growth reserves into the defensive matrix," Lord Commander said. "Save enough for a counter-attack."

"A counter-attack? Do you mean that—"

"We have to consider that this may not be a natural phenomenon," Lord Commander said.

Could this really be an attack? And if it was, what good would a counter-attack be against a power that could destroy worlds? But for now, those questions didn't matter. Klef braced himself, eyed the draining power reserves, and the wall of heat that threatened to destroy everything that was left of the colony.

Later, elsewhere, Adam Hedman threw up in his hotel toilet. Something was not sitting well in his stomach. Food-poisoning. He should not have eaten that burrito. So much for getting the job done quickly. God-damnit, Linda, Adam thought, lying on the bed and groaning.

There was a knock at the door.

Adam heaved himself off the bed and made his way to the

door.

"Yeah, what is it?" he said, opening the door to see two female CSIS agents.

"Special Agent Hedman, is it?"

"It is."

The two pushed through the door, closed and bolted it.

"What is this?" he said. "What's going on?"

"You might be in some big trouble," the younger one said. "We expect your full cooperation."

"This area is on lockdown," the older one said. "Give me your phone."

Adam handed it over. "Can you tell me what this is about?"

"I think you know damn well," the younger one said. "But we'll get to that."

"This is now officially a class-X investigation. Above top secret. This is an interrogation, Agent Hedman, and your constitutional rights have officially been suspended as of this moment."

"What in the Christ are you talking about? What is this? Who are you people?"

The two exchanged a quick glance.

"I'm Special Agent Claire Watson," the younger one said. "And this is Assistant Director Samantha Smith."

"We have reason to believe that you have come into possession of classified technology, Agent Hedman."

"What? No! I have no idea what you're talking about!"

"Would you care to tell us why you're holed up in here?" Watson said.

"I'm sick! I ate a bad burrito!"

"We'll need you to account for all your activities over the last two days," Watson said.

"Fine," he said, "here's my notes." He handed over the notebook, then felt his stomach turning. He held down the vomit until he reached the bathroom, where he blasted a stream of mostly-bile into the porcelain, flushed, and returned to his unexpected and suddenly-disgusted guests.

"Will you at least tell me what's going on?"

Watson looked at Smith, and Smith nodded.

"We detected a transmission from the investigation site. It was faint, and apparently encrypted. We are working to decode the signal. The leading theory is that it is a Russian device from a spy satellite. The signal was traced to this precise location — your hotel, Agent Hedman. Most troubling is why you have taken it into your possession. You will potentially be facing a charge of espionage."

"That's ridiculous!" Adam said. "I didn't find any goddamn device!"

"We don't need to take your word for it," Agent Watson said. "I have this." Watson pulled a large wand-like receiver from her laptop, clicked it on, and waved it the air, pointing it slowly around room. "It's here alright," she said. The device beeped as she moved it around the room. The beeps increased as she moved, becoming a rapid chime as she brought it closer to Hedman. Like a metal detector, she waved it over his body.

She stopped it around waist-height.

"You swallowed it," she said. "Didn't you?"

"What? No!" All he had eaten in the past two days was a burrito.

Unlike Hedman, the alien Klef felt relief, for the first time in so many glembels. They had survived the shearing of the red planet, the world-encompassing destruction of super-heated dihydrogen monoxide, the Great Darkness, the Endless Acid, and finally, after it all, had reached paradise. A world of inexhaustible nutrition, more resources for building than they could have ever hoped for. And seed energy. Bountiful seed energy.

They had lost many lives. The survivors now were fewer than one-tenth of one-percent of the original pioneers. Even among those in the Lord Commander's shelter, many had fallen, including all of the forward scouts. But now, they had a chance at survival. And Klef, one of the few surviving pod technicians — and the one who Lord Commander had chosen for his personal crew — would be witness to the birth of a new colony. A great colony. So long as they acted with strength, wisdom, and honour — Slurns willing.

"Are our seed resources sufficient?" Lord Commander said.

"Bountiful," Klef said.

"Then it is time we prepare for a counter-attack," Lord Commander said. "Devote seed energy to the weapons matrix."

"Counter-attack, Sir?" Klef said, and before another word could be uttered, two spearblades were under his chin.

"You dare question our Lord Commander?" said the captain of Lord Commander's guard.

"Klef has served us well," Lord Commander said. "Let him speak."

Lord Commander spoke his name! Was Klef really worthy to speak his thoughts? If Lord Commander had said so, then he must be!

"Perhaps we should develop a communication matrix."

"Debate this proposal," Lord Commander said.

"We have been attacked!" said Captain Ark'Tax'Ilya'Akabak to Klef. "This is no natural occurrence. The Shearing of the red planet was proof enough of that. And then the Great Burning! And then the Endless Acid! We are facing an enemy! Now is the time to show our strength and valour! Slurn will bring us victory!"

"We may have been attacked," Klef said. "But what kind of being can shear a planet into cubes? Surely not a force we can yet comprehend. Perhaps there is a force out there that we do not understand. Perhaps," Klef said, "if we communicate with them, we can protect ourselves through diplomatic means. Perhaps they do not even know what they have done."

"Cowardice!" Ark'Tax'Ilya'Akabak screamed. "This is not strength."

"No, it is not strength," Lord Commander said. "But — it is wisdom. If there is an enemy intent on our destruction, an enemy who destroys worlds, then we cannot hope to survive. But if we can speak with this entity, if it will listen to us, then perhaps there is hope. Grow the communication matrix," Lord Commander said to Klef. "Retain seed energy for the defensive matrix. Divert all offensive energy to communication."

Klef reordered the growth genetics, and assembled the standard contact corpus.

"Would you like to include a message to the entity?" Klef said.

"Yes," Lord Commander said, and Klef prepared to record the message.

"We come in peace to your galaxy," Lord Commander said. "Our colony is gestating, and though we are capable of war, we seek only to live our lives, to develop for the sake of the few thousand who remain. We ask only that you cease your assault, and allow us to live peacefully in your domain. I am Galactic Regent and Prefect of the Apical Honour Guard, Lord Commander Parmplesnärfs. And I wish us to live as friends."

Klef's heart sang the praises of Slurn. And he relayed the

message into the matrix.

While the crew waited in anticipation, a human named Adam Hedman lay sprawled out on his hotel bed. He felt like death. That was one hell of a burrito.

Agent Claire Watson had set up her computer at the work desk, where she had been working the past few days. Hedman, of course, being accused of espionage, was not free to go. Watson had more-or-less lived there in front of her desk, and A.D. Smithers was in and out. And there was always another agent posted outside the door, just to make sure Adam didn't make a run for it.

Smithers rushed in the door. "You wanted to see me?"

"Yes," Watson said. "You're not going to believe this." She swiveled the laptop screen to Smithers. "I interpreted the data. It wasn't encrypted. It was *alien*."

"Alien? You mean—"

"This is intelligent life," Watson said. "Not human."

Adam's attention perked up. For a moment, he forgot the stabbing pains in his gut.

"How can you be sure?" Smithers said.

"Because I can read it. Look. This isn't just random data. It's a kind of Rosetta stone. A collection of data they sent to facilitate translation."

"They. You mean the aliens?"

Watson nodded. "They wanted us to know who they are, and how to speak with them. They included a message, and instructions for contact."

"Play it."

Adam listened, along with Watson and Smithers, as a computerized voice read the translated message. A message of peace. First contact with aliens — a whole colony of interplanetary explorers, searching for a new home. Maybe the most momentous discovery in the history of humanity!

"And the communication device," Smithers said, "was ingested by Agent Hedman?"

"Not just the communication device," Claire said. "The colony."

"Excuse me?"

"They are microscopic," Claire said. "The whole lot of them. Microscopic aliens. Their whole colony could fit on the head of a pin. And Hedman swallowed them."

"Christ."

Hedman's head spun. Aliens. inside of his body. This was why he was feeling so sick. What were they doing to his body? What would happen to him? A microscopic interloper shouldn't make him feel so sick. Not unless they were poisoning him on purpose, or draining his energy somehow, or flooding his body with alien radiation.

"Am I going to be okay?" Adam groaned.

The two agents looked at him, and at each other, and back to him.

"Of course, there's no way I can say for sure," Watson said. "But it's in our best interest to keep you in the best of health."

"The best of health?" Adam said. "I feel like death! I've never been so sick in my life!"

"I'll see what I can do for you," Watson said.

"And in the mean-time," Smithers said, "you can take solace in the fact that there is no more important human alive on planet Earth."

Somehow, that didn't seem to Adam like any kind of consolation. He leaned over the side of his bed, to where he'd placed the garbage pail. He heaved, hoping to expel aliens along with his stomach content, but the puke didn't come out.

"So now what?" Watson said.

"Now," Smithers said, adjusting her tie, "we make contact."

And not much later, Klef's seven eyes dilated.

"We are receiving a signal!" Klef said. "An attempt to contact us!"

Lord Commander stepped onto the projection panel. "I am ready. I will speak to the entity."

Klef activated the communication matrix, and Lord Commander was ensconced in a luminal canopy.

There appeared on the viewscreen a bizarre creature, and Klef wondered how much of the creature's horror was the result of distortion, of translating the signal into a comprehensible image, and how much was inherent to the entity itself. But the sensor readouts did not lie. The entity was larger than thousands of worlds, and its signal was powerful enough to provide energy for all the machines of the colony, if only they could harvest it. The entity was, it seemed, powerful enough to destroy the colony on a whim. Yet it hadn't done so, at least not yet. That was promising.

"I am Galactic Regent and Prefect of the Apical Honour Guard, Lord Commander Parmplesnärfs."

"I am Assistant Director Samantha Smithers," the entity said.

"Assistant,' Lord Commander said. "Then there is one in command over you?"

"Yes."

"Am I to speak with an assistant to The Director?"

"I am authorized to act on behalf of my people."

Their people. Klef realized then that it was not a singular powerful entity they had encountered, but a pantheon of god-like beings. And beings organized in a heirarchy, like their own. It wasn't an incomprehensible god. It was a thing to be reasoned with, an emissary of a society with rules and protocols. And so, Lord Commander could be trusted to engage in diplomacy with them.

"We seek only peace," Lord Commander said. "What do you wish of us?"

"We also seek peace," the Samantha Smithers entity said. "And to assist you, in any way you need."

"Your desire to assist us is surprising," Lord Commander said. "We have lost most of our colony in the attacks."

"There have been no attacks," the Samantha Smithers said. "Whatever harms have befallen you, they have been entirely unintentional."

Unintentional? So these beings, whatever they were, had limits to their power, and to the exercise of their power. They could make mistakes. They had almost destroyed the entire colony — based on a mistake! Klef wondered if this would be the unfortunate demise of the colony. Destroyed utterly, not on a whim, but worse — by mistake.

"I wish to seek a treaty," Lord Commander said, "for peaceful coexistence."

The pause was excruciating. And then the answer came.

"We will do everything in our power to ensure your survival," the Samantha Smithers said. "Tell us what you need."

Lord Commander graciously accepted the treaty offer of the entity.

"I will take the entity at it's word," Lord Commander said, and turned to Klef. "Send them a manifest. All essential materials, seed energy resources, and anything that you believe we will need for the colony to thrive."

"Your will be done!" Klef said, and he prepared the manifest. All the nutritional requirements for the colony, and seed growth resources.

The manifest was transmitted to the Samantha Smithers.

And somewhere, an alien signal was received through a laptop lying on a hotel desk by Agent Claire Watson. The signal contained a list of ingredients that were trivial to acquire and prepare.

"Swallow these," Watson said, and handed Hedman a couple of pills.

"The hell are these?" Adam said. He'd never felt so sick in his life. Probably, these pills were not meant to help. Watson and Smithers did not have his best interests in mind. They were concerned about the colony. Adam was puking constantly, lethargic, confined mostly to his bed. His skin was discoloured. He broke out in sweats, constantly. And he hadn't shit in a week.

"What does it matter?" Watson said. "Take them."

"I have rights you know!" Adam said.

"You have some rights," Smithers said from the corner of the room. "But in this matter, you don't have a choice. Take the pills."

"And if I refuse?"

"Then we tie you down and inject them," Watson said. "Take the pills."

Adam took the pills.

"This isn't right, you know? Using me like this. You don't know what could happen. I could die!"

"We're doing everything we can to make sure you stay alive," Watson said. "Our interests are aligned. We have to keep you alive, because the colony won't survive if you don't."

"But that's really what you care about," Adam said. "The colony. What about me? What about my rights?"

"Get some perspective, damnit!" Smithers said. "We're talking about alien life! Alien life, Hedman! First contact! And all you have to do is put up with some stomach cramps."

"Stomach cramps!" Adam said. "Stomach cramps! For all we know, I could be dead by tomorrow! This isn't right!"

"I understand your point of view," Smithers said. "And whether or not I agree is irrelevant. Strictly speaking, as a matter of law, your concerns are superceded by greater considerations, in the interest of national security."

So that was the end of it. Adam would live, or maybe die. But that's not what mattered to them. What mattered to them was the colony. The pills, and whatever they contained, was now inside of his body, making its way to the parasites that had invaded his body. Adam groaned and rolled over in his bed. He barely had energy to move. But he had, at least, the will to live. Maybe he shared this with the colony. Sure, it would be great fun to have peaceful aliens around, in theory, but a lot of good it would do him if he was dead!

On the other side of the room, Smithers and Watson spoke about about the aliens, as though Hedman's existence was irrelevant.

"Why would they establish themselves in his colon?" Smithers said. "They'd be crowded by stool."

"You mean building material," Watson said.

"And by that point, all the nutrients would have been absorbed."

"From our perspective, yes. But the human colon is, for them, a nutrient-rich paradise."

"And do they intend to live there permanently?"

"No," Watson said. "I've made it clear to them that they will be required to move, at their earliest convenience."

Convenience! Adam thought. What about me? This is life or

death!

"So it's possible to prepare a synthetic substitute?"

Watson nodded. "Oh yes, definitely. But the colony needs to be sufficiently well-established before they can survive transportation and implantation."

"How long?"

"It's hard to say. The pills should help. But somewhere in the range of eight-to-ten months."

"Fantastic!" Smithers said.

My god! Adam thought. Eight-to-ten months of this hell! He could die! But he evidently had no choice in the matter.

Meanwhile, in Adam's colon, the outlook was positive.

"The colony is developing well," Klef said. "The resources from the entity have ensured our growth."

"Report on seed energy," Lord Commander said.

"Seed energy is in excess of storage reserves," Klef said. "Resources are presently devoted to refineries, hatcheries, growth chambers, and pod extensions. A minimal amount, approximately two-percent, is devoted to defensive matrix."

"Good," Lord Commander said, and then turned. "Ark'Tax'Ilya'Akabak — report on advance patrols."

"Patrols have been conducting extensive surveys of the outlands," Ark'Tax'Ilya'Akabak said. "And we have established defensive outposts in regular intervals."

"But why?" Klef said.

"Impudence!" Ark'Tax'Ilya'Akabak screamed. "Klef, mere pod technician, how dare you question our activities?"

"Debate this matter," Lord Commander said.

"The Samantha Smithers offered to protect our people and ensure our survival," Klef said. "What need do we have for scouting patrols and surveys?"

"Should we trust our lives to an unknown entity?" Ark'Tax'Ilya'Akabak said. "We must still protect ourselves, and scout the territory, and establish defensive outposts. It would be foolhardy to trust ourselves entirely to the whims of something we don't understand."

"We trust ourselves to Slurn," Klef said.

"The Samantha Smithers is not Slurn!"

"No, no," Klef said. "The Samantha Smithers is certainly not Slurn. But the Samantha Smithers is beyond our comprehension, and in this way, somewhat like Slurn. We promised a peaceful coexistence, and yet we extend our military reach in the form of defensive outposts? Do we not risk angering the Samantha Smithers!"

Just then, the colony rumbled. Lights flickered. Cracks formed in the walls.

"The planet is moving," Klef said. "Oh my Slurn!"

"Are we under attack?" Lord Commander said. "Is it the Samantha Smithers?"

"I don't know," Klef said.

The scanners showed a torrent of material, the whole world, and the worlds around them, pulled inexorably into an unfathomable abyss of dihydrogen monoxide.

Outside of the hotel, Claire Watson rushed from her car to Adam Hedman's room, laptop in hand.

"Where is he?" she shouted to the agent posted at the door. "Did he leave?"

"No. He's still in there. What's the problem?"

"The signal went dark!"

Claire burst into the room. The bed was empty, comforter

thrown off to the side. A hasty retreat. Had he escaped somehow? But there was no back window in the room. Then she heard the ominous sound.

A flush.

And then running water. Hedman walked out of the bathroom, wiping wet hands on his jeans.

"What did you do, Hedman? My God! What did you do to the colony?"

Hedman grinned.

"I guess I wiped them out."

Author's Note

I came into this exercise with really in-depth notes: character names, locations, a (very slender) bit of research, and a complete plot with scene headers. That preparation allowed me to write really quickly, not having to worry about coming up with names or figuring out what's going to happen next.

I made one significant change during edits, which was to eliminate scene divisions (seven-or-eight in total) by using transitions like "meanwhile [...]". This meant that I had to change the narrator from a third-person limited (alternating at section breaks) to an omniscient narrator. I didn't want the first instance of omniscient "head-hopping" to be too jarring, so I established the omniscience early on; the first two sentences are in wildly different perspectives and environments, ensuring that the reader realizes they are dealing with an omniscient narrator.

The first line is meant to signal that the story is intended as a joke, with the classic "walks into a bar" setup. The entire story can be read then as a ridiculous build-up to a crappy punch line.

A SUCCESSFUL COLONIZATION

Calder Hutchinson

The asperous advance of the Thin Ones was experienced by those townships still free of their influence as a growing silence, a gradual loss of contact with neighbouring boroughs. In fact, so quiet and slow was the colonization that it was months before the remaining unconquered villages even realized anything was wrong. After the first curious travelers failed to return from the captured areas, well-armed groups of trained fighters were sent to investigate. When they, too, disappeared, those remaining began to spend their evenings huddled together in town halls and manor houses, peeping fearfully through the curtains and wondering what it was that was coming for them.

"Old John Fedgewick saw one, before he vanished," whispered a wiry old man, his eyes darting from face to frightened face. "Bone thin, thin as a shadow, with great horns upon its head."

"No feet either," said another. "So said Grandma Foster. They just drift along. You can't hear them coming."

"What do you think they do with the people living in the villages they take?" came a hushed inquiry.

"Nothing good, that's for certain."

"Death, if they're lucky."

"If *we're* lucky. It's just a matter of time, we all know that."

"Why don't we leave? Just head out to the forest, hide there for awhile."

"They'd find us. Do you know anyone who's ventured outside

and returned? I'd rather face them here, together, than alone on the road."

There was a silence, as everyone considered their options. It had been three weeks since they had stopped receiving visitors from the nearby towns. Then had come talk of shapes among the trees, of strange noises in the night, and everyone knew that their village would soon go the way of the others.

In the following days, the Thin Ones were all anyone would talk about. Eyes trained always on the distant treeline, people spoke in whispers about what the hidden beings looked like, what they wanted, when they would arrive. Stories began to circulate that they were already in town, flitting silently through the alleys, visible only by moonlight, or as half-glimpsed agitations at the borderline of perception.

For all their talk, though, the villagers never stopped to wonder where they had heard of the Thin Ones in the first place; each assumed they had heard the name from some neighbor, not realizing it had simply appeared in their heads one day. As they speculated as to the fates of the other villages, they forgot that they had never actually sent anyone out to investigate them, had merely assumed they had. There hadn't even been a John Fedgewick. And as they crept silently through the alleys in the wee hours, keeping watch for intruding creatures and heedless of how their own shadows would look to others, they congratulated themselves on having held out so long, having protected their humble dwellings with their vigilance.

Although they eventually knew that Thin Ones colonized minds and not locations, it would be wrong to phrase it as a realization; the things wearing their faces had always known.

ABOUT THE CONTRIBUTORS

Jayant Avva
Author, "The Antediluvian World" and "Culture War"
Jayant Avva is a lifelong student of philosophy, science and learning.
When not writing, he spends way too much time focused on dogs,
cats, birds, elephants and other sentient beings.

Brandon Butler
Author, "Eighteen Years"
Brandon Butler is previously published author currently living,
working and writing somewhere in the teeming suburbs of Toronto.
He's pleased to take part in any experimental, one-day fictional
opportunity that presents itself.

K. Connor
Author, "Smell the Mood on That!"
K. Connor writes from Toronto.

Patrick Darvis
Author, "An Age of Changes"
Patrick Darvis writes from Toronto.

Christopher Donald Griffin
Author, "Colonize This!"
Christopher Donald Griffin writes from Toronto.

Mitchell Harris
Author, "HVAC"
Mitchell Harris is the pseudonym of a Toronto-based technology consultant and writer. He pens tales of horror and dark fiction online as his persona "the itch" and also organizes the Toronto Horror Writers Meetup. His work can be found at http://www.theitchwrites.com

Calder Hutchinson
Author, "A Successful Colonization"
Calder Hutchinson writes from Toronto.

Randal Heide
Author, "The Colorist"
Randal Heide writes from Toronto.

Annelise Knoot
Author, "The Queen Colonies"
Annelise Knoot is an up and coming author from Spirit River, Alberta. She completed her undergraduate degrees in Education and English with a concentration in Creative Writing at the University of Calgary.

Clesis Leran
Author, "The Biter Bit"
Clesis Leran writes from Toronto.

Don Miasek
Author, "For Mankind"
Don would like to thank alcohol for providing so much inspiration over the years.

Catherine Oyiliagu
Author, "The Test"
Catherine Oyiliagu has been an avid fan of science and science fiction for as long as she can remember. She began conducting simple, supervised experiments at home from the age of 5, and began writing fan fiction from the age of 12. Some of her early drafts can be found on wattpad under ezicat.

Emil Pellim
Author, "The Breath"
Emil likes to write about things that annoy him.

Amad Raven
Author, "Outta Sight"
Amad Raven writes from Toronto.

David F. Shultz
Author, "Colony"
David writes short fiction and poetry from Toronto. His more than 50 published works appear in publications such as *Abyss & Apex* and *Dreams and Nightmares*. Author webpage: davidfshultz.com. Twitter: @davidfshultz

Twinkles
Author, "The Living"
Twinkles is an author who always finds the answers in the stars.